A summer of witches

(A Molly Morgan adventure)

by M. Ganendran

Prologue

1780

The rain beat mercilessly down across the rolling landscape, running in rivulets across the heathland and pooling up in dips and crevices. A lone figure swathed in a dark cloak laboured its way along the Smugglers Road, criss-crossing towards Vereley Hill.

"Wait, wait, whoa! Cut! You're not starting it off like *that* are you?"
"What's wrong with it? I need to set the scene"
"But it's just so *predictable*. A dark night, rain pouring down, a shadowy figure…"
"But that's the way it **was.** I'm the one writing this, so can you please be quiet and let me get on with the story? You're spoiling the atmosphere."

I'm sorry about that. My writing colleague, as he likes to call himself, keeps interrupting. I haven't had a chance to introduce him yet, or even myself, come to think of it. That comes later. Anyway, where was I?

The rain beat mercilessly down across the rolling landscape, running in rivulets across the heathland and pooling up in dips and crevices. A lone figure swathed in a dark cloak laboured its way along the Smugglers Road, criss-crossing towards Vereley Hill.

The relentless precipitation made progress slow, and the figure hunched forwards to protect its face from the stinging pellets of rain.

Once, the traveller stumbled, falling into the mud before regaining weary legs.

Eventually arriving at journey's end, the figure flung open the door of the Queen's Head Public House in the New Forest village of Burley, and the soaked hood was pulled back to reveal a woman with drenched, matted hair and a face filled with terror. The patrons of the inn turned at the sound of the new arrival and their jovial chatter and the clattering of tankards fell quiet.

"For god's sake, hide it! Hide it all now! If you value your lives, make ready and be gone, for the excise men are coming!" she cried, eyes wild.
Stunned silence reigned for a moment and then uproar followed. Stools and mugs of ale were upended in the haste to hide any evidence of contraband.
The landlord leapt over the bar, shouting for the men to follow him.
"There's a hidden cellar round the back of the Stable Bar! Come quickly, you blackguards!"

They scurried back and forth, cursing as they desperately tossed flintlocks, coins and bottles into the secret chamber. Just a few hours earlier on the coast, they had taken delivery of barrels full of smuggled goods from the Isle of Wight, and their merry caravan had travelled to the public house in celebratory mood for the horses to rest overnight before the onward journey upcountry. The premises and their carts were full to bursting. Some men raced outside to unload crates of tea and gin from the wagons, while others darted into the night to keep watch for the approaching government men. An owl hooted and the rain pelted the ground harder and faster, as the darkness transformed into a dangerous threat rather than a safe cover.

The woman who had run so tirelessly to warn them was not yet ready to rest. She frantically searched the inn, voice wavering as she called out for someone.
"Jeremiah! Jeremiah, where are you? Are you here?"
The thud of horses' hooves on the cobblestones was deafening as the excise men approached. The woman turned with a start as a tall, broad man with a strong jaw and fair, curly hair laid a calloused hand on her shoulder.
"Jeremiah! Thank god, there you are! Get out of here quickly, you must hurry!"
"Sister, I thank you for coming to warn us. How did you know?"
"There's no time! I overheard Uncle sending a rider to tell the government men. He's betrayed you all Jeremiah, he can no longer be trusted!"

They jumped at the nearby sound of shots, cowering as a melange of startled cries and whinnying of horses broke out.
"Sarah, I must go. I'll distract the horsemen, and perchance some of the others may be able to escape. If anything befalls me, I beg that you and Thomas look after Mary and the children."
"Jeremiah! No!"
But he had already gritted his teeth and was running heedlessly into the fray, firing musket shots into the air.

Sarah shook as she watched from behind a cask in the shadows of the inn, unable to tear her eyes away from her brother. He was intentionally putting himself in harm's way, shouting mockeries to distract the hated excise men, to prevent them from noticing the other smugglers who were creeping off into the night through the back door, leaving nothing but empty wagons behind them.

It was only a few moments before Jeremiah was clapped in irons and the destructive ransacking of the inn began, the din of smashing glass and thudding tables accompanying the search for evidence of contraband. But his swift action had granted the rest of the gang precious time to make their escape and vanish into the night. A few excise men gave half-hearted pursuit but it was too late; the other smugglers had melted away like shadows, along with the inn-keeper who had no wish to face charges for harbouring criminals.

Tears mingled with the rain water streaming down Sarah's dirt-streaked face as her mind conjured terrible images of her brother's fate. Despite his illicit smuggling activities, he had never harmed a soul in his life, and had not intended to do so today, merely shooting into the air to create a diversion and allow his comrades a chance to evade capture.
He often gave away a portion of his spoils to the poor in the village who would otherwise have struggled to pay the high prices. He was a good man. Would he be imprisoned? With certainty. Would he hang? It was likely.

The vigorous smashing of crates and splintering of wooden chairs startled her, prompting her to make her own getaway, so she gathered her skirts and crept quietly off into the darkness to begin the long journey home through the mud and rain once more, her thoughts preoccupied by how she would break the news to her brother's wife and children.

As he tossed and turned amongst the fetid straw in his squalid cell that night, plagued by nightmares of the hangman's noose, Jeremiah was terrified yet resigned to his fate. The one thing that had given him a small taste of bittersweet amusement was overhearing two guards murmuring in disappointment that the excise men had gone empty-handed, unable to find the hidden stash of smuggled goods at the Queen's Head. He closed his eyes and wished he could rub his ankles, made sore by the shackles, or at least give his cramped arms a stretch. Yet he didn't regret his actions. How many of his friends had been saved by his quick thinking? Perhaps he was a fool to have risked his life in this way, but he didn't think so. "It's alright" he whispered to himself, cursing that he had no free hand to wipe the sweat-soaked lock of hair from his eyes. "It's alright. My work isn't yet done. The wheel must still come full circle, and one day I will be able to help someone again".

Chapter 1

1940

“Where d’you think we’re going then?”
The girl’s voice grated in his ears, rousing him from his thoughts. Lawrence looked up with a sigh, taking in his carriage partner. She looked about 12, the same as him, and had hair as black as molasses that seemed to go on forever, framing a pale and chiselled face. Her piercing green eyes bore into him.
“Well?” she prompted him.
“I don’t know” he reluctantly answered with a shrug. “There are lots of little villages out here. I don’t much care.”
He drew his eyebrows together and blinked rapidly as if he might be trying to prevent himself from crying.

Feeling awkward, the girl turned to look out of the window at the passing fields, and for a moment she was quiet and all that could be heard was the regular clacking and chugging of the steam train as it laboured its way through the countryside.
Not to be silenced for long, she soon piped up again. “What’s your name?”
She reached for his name tag before he could answer. “Oh, Lawrence. I’m Rachel. Not much like Portsmouth round here, is it?”
She tugged at her own tag in annoyance.

“No” Lawrence answered softly, realising he wasn’t going to be allowed to sit quietly in his sorrows while this troublesome girl occupied the same compartment.

"But my m-mother and father always say it's healthy to get fresh air away from town anyway." He sniffed, voice wavering at the mention of his parents whom he missed dreadfully already.
"I just wish I had my sketchbook and pens with me" he added.
"Weren't you allowed to bring them?"
"I left them behind in all the rush. I nearly forgot my gas mask and mother was running up and down stairs looking for it, and we thought I might miss the train and… well, they were on the kitchen table and I forgot to pick them up."

He looked embarrassed at having given such a long speech and looked down at his feet with reddened cheeks.
"I wish I *had* missed the train" he added in a murmur.
"Me too" Rachel burst out. "I'd rather take a chance on the bombs back home than be stuck out here! Who knows what kind of people we'll end up with?"

Lawrence had been worried about this himself.
"Maybe the war will be over by the end of the summer" he whispered quietly, more to reassure himself than Rachel.
"Maybe" she replied. "But in any case, I should think you'd rather have your gas mask than your sketchbook".

Lawrence was unconvinced. After a moment, he noticed his stomach was rumbling and remembered that it had been a long time since breakfast.

Unbuttoning the satchel that each child had been given at the station, he found a tin of corned beef, a can of carnation milk and a bar of chocolate. As he hungrily ripped open the latter, he thought regretfully of his mother's lunches, lovingly prepared each day and ready on the table when he walked home from the morning's lessons, warming and filling to keep him going for the trudge back to school for the afternoon. He was a rather quiet child who occupied himself for hours with books and drawing, and was naturally apprehensive about how he would settle into a different home, neighbourhood and school. His stomach lurched as he thought about what awaited him, and he wished he hadn't eaten the chocolate bar after all.

Glancing up, he noticed that Rachel had followed suit and was tucking into her own bar.
"Not much good giving us a tin of corned beef, is it?" she observed with her mouth full, "without a tin opener".
Despite himself, Lawrence laughed, realising that perhaps it was better to be speaking to someone after all. After all, they were in exactly the same situation.

Before long they felt the train slowing. Both children craned their necks out of the window but saw nothing except fields full of horses.
"They're not just going to dump us in the middle of nowhere are they? Do you think they'll make us build tree-houses or sleep outside?" asked Rachel, only half-joking.

“Don’t be silly” Lawrence answered, feeling grumpy as anxiety crept over him again. “It feels like we’re pulling in now.”

As they chugged into the tiny station, they saw that the name was Holmsley.
“Never heard of it” Rachel shrugged.
Lawrence hadn’t either.
There was a rather old but kindly looking vicar waiting for them on the platform with a cluster of women behind him, who looked almost as nervous as the children felt.

As Lawrence and Rachel stepped off the train clutching their tiny suitcases and satchels, it became clear that every evacuee had been allocated to a local family who had agreed to take them in for the duration of the war. Fifty children haphazardly selected from two or three schools had been sent here; others would have gone further west to Somerset or Devon and perhaps others east to the Sussex or Kent countryside. There didn’t seem to be much method to the allocations and all the officials were simply swept up in the panic of getting as many children out of the vulnerable towns and cities as possible.

“Alright, gather round!” the vicar called with a frazzled half-smile, exhausted from greeting trainloads of evacuees every day for the past week. “I’ll read out your names and announce which lady you’re to go with. The lady in question will wave her hand, and you’re to make your way quietly over to her with your luggage, and she’ll take you home to your billet”.

He rustled a sheet of paper and coughed. “I’m sure you’ll all be on your best behaviour” he added hopefully.

The gaggle of children was unusually quiet as the list was read, and all bravado fell away from even the most garrulous as each one arrived at the unsettling realisation that they were far away from home and had no idea what to expect, and when, or *if*, they would see their families again. Some had looked on the train journey as something of an adventure, but now the cold reality was sinking in.
Lawrence and Rachel were the last ones to be called. They stood awkwardly on the platform, noticing that there was only one woman still waiting for her evacuee. They thought she looked rather forbidding, thin nose and sharp features making her look older than she probably was. Her hair was streaked with grey and secured tightly in a bun, and she was dressed in a long skirt and a blouse covered by a crocheted shawl in spite of the warm weather.

The vicar consulted his list and a frown crossed his face.
“Th- there seems to be some sort of mix-up” he stuttered. “I’m afraid Rachel here has been put on the wrong train – she should have gone to Blandford Forum.”
“I can only take one” the stern woman snapped. “I already told you I don’t have enough room.”
The vicar was embarrassed but tried appealing to her better nature.

“I really am sorry, Mrs Fernley. But when these problems arise, there’s nothing we can do. We can’t very well send the young lady on another train alone, and besides, a mix-up may have occurred at the other end too and there mightn’t be a home for her there either. Is there really no way you could - ?” he trailed off hopefully.
Mrs Fernley scowled.
“I was only meant to take one. The boy”
Lawrence and Rachel held their breath.
“I suppose I’ll have to take her too” she made no effort to hide her irritation. “But it really won’t do. I’ll do my bit for the war effort in the meantime but it would be best if alternative arrangements can be made”.
The vicar, visibly relieved, praised and flattered Mrs Fernley unceasingly and ushered the children towards her as quickly as possible, lest she changed her mind. His duty now discharged, he hurried off, knowing that even if he lodged a request for the girl to be moved elsewhere, everyone was so busy organising evacuations that there wouldn’t be an opportunity to arrange it. He would let the matter rest unless Mrs Fernley pestered him about it again.

Lawrence and Rachel glanced at each other nervously. Although they had only met on the train for the first time a short while ago, each of them felt grateful to be with the other as it seemed just a little less daunting than being sent into a whole new life completely alone. Mrs Fernley strode on ahead, making an occasional remark or barking a terse instruction with barely a glance back at the children trailing along behind.

They clambered into her dented old Austin as she unceremoniously bundled their small cases inside. The car lurched and jolted and Lawrence and Rachel were soon feeling nauseous. Mrs Fernley drove for about a mile and a half, before reaching the small New Forest village of Burley, surrounded by trees and smattered with a few shops. The area seemed almost deserted apart from an elderly man entering the post office, and two small donkeys standing at the side of the road looking rather bored. To the children, animals roaming loose were an unfamiliar sight. A large white cross stood proudly in the centre of a grassy patch.

"What's that for?" Rachel dared to ask, trying to distract herself as she was feeling very green about the gills thanks to the bumpy ride.
"Memorial for those killed in the First World War" Mrs Fernley replied brusquely. "And no doubt many more will die in this one".
Discouraged from making further conversation, the children remained silent until they pulled up outside a pretty country cottage, clothed in ivy and fronted by a garden bursting with colourful flowers.

Relieved to be standing safely on firm ground after the brief but bone-shaking journey, Lawrence wanted to remark on the beauty of the garden but felt too shy to say anything.
His parents both enjoyed gardening but they didn't have much space back in Portsmouth. He knew how much they would have loved this, and he was forced once again to squeeze his eyes shut to stem the tears that came so easily when he thought of home.

Mrs Fernley gestured for the children to follow her inside. The cottage wasn't large but if its ambition in life was to make its inhabitants feel unwelcome, then it was certainly succeeding. It was surprisingly draughty, and was evidently less well cared for than the garden. A curving set of stairs led up from the small entrance hall, and Lawrence and Rachel noticed how bare everything looked with very few ornaments, and rather thin, moth-eaten rugs limply covering the stone floor. A fly buzzed half-heartedly above them and there was a faint smell of stewed vegetables in the air.

"Well, this is your home for now" Mrs Fernley announced. "I've no interest in children so you can occupy yourselves, so long as you don't get into any trouble and don't bother me. I work as a clerk at a doctor's surgery in Ringwood so I shall be out of the house for most of the day from Monday to Friday, and often Saturday mornings too. I was granted leave today to collect you."
"Thank you" Lawrence thought it wise to acknowledge Mrs Fernley's kindness in taking them in. His comment was ignored as their hostess launched into a series of staccato commands.

"Breakfast is at seven in the morning, and dinner is seven at night. I will prepare your lunch and leave it in the pantry for you. You will eat what you are given and like it. You are to keep out of my way and stay silent in your rooms after nine o'clock. Please refrain from touching my belongings or meddling with anything in this house. Lawrence, your room is the first on the left upstairs. You, girl – what was your name?"

"Rachel" she answered softly; despite her urge to rebel at being addressed so harshly, she thought it wise to remain as docile as possible for now.

"Rachel, you'll have to sleep in my late husband's study. I'll arrange bedding for you today but it won't be comfortable. All his things are still there and are not to be touched under any circumstances. Do I make myself clear to both of you?" her eagle eyes darted between them.

"Yes, Mrs Fernley" they answered, overwhelmed by the unwelcoming tirade.

After they had unpacked their few belongings, washed their faces, combed their hair and surrendered their ration books on Mrs Fernley's orders, they found their way outside through the kitchen door to the secluded back garden, shaded by giant trees and peppered with rose bushes.

Overhanging weeping willows gently grazed the grass in the breeze and the peaceful, soporific buzz of a bee created a sleepy summer background hum.
The friendly, peaceful nature of the garden was a complete antithesis to the Spartan furnishings and tense atmosphere of the house. The children couldn't imagine Mrs Fernley being the patient architect of this glorious outdoor paradise and decided she must employ a gardener.

"So, this is our new home" Rachel said as they sat cross-legged on the grass. "It could be worse I suppose."
"Could it?"
"It's like she just isn't interested in us and will leave us alone, but some children might be unlucky and end up with someone really horrid".
"Mm" Lawrence didn't feel much like talking.
"She might be alright when we get used to her", Rachel continued. "But she is a bit of an old battle-axe!" She snorted in laugher as she plucked daisies to make a chain. She pursed her lips and narrowed her eyes in impersonation of their hostess.
"You are to keep out of my way at all times, and children must be seen and not heard. You'll eat what you're given and like it, whether it's stale bread and water or not!" she mimicked Mrs Fernley's peevish tone.
Despite his sadness, Lawrence couldn't resist chuckling, but stifled it quickly, looking up in horror. Rachel's face fell as she turned to discover Mrs Fernley looming over them with an even crosser expression on her face than usual.
"You'll get nothing to eat at all if you take that attitude" she barked. "Dinner's on the table".

The meal was a silent affair but satisfying despite the rationing; corned beef fritters with carrot and potato mash, followed by apple crumble. Afterwards, both children thanked Mrs Fernley in genuine appreciation, but felt liberated from the awkward silence around the dinner table when they retreated back outdoors to make the most of the last light. Whether it was due to their full stomachs or the fresh countryside air laced with the heady scent of myriad flowers, they each began to feel a little more optimistic. It was one of those rare, glittering moments in life when despite all your troubles you somehow manage to grasp a little slice of the rainbow, quite by chance, and with a certain atmosphere and a particular trick of the light, and a little warm spark inside, you begin to feel that everything just *might* turn out alright, after all.

"It's summer, anyhow" Rachel smiled. "No school! We'll be by ourselves for most of the day so we can do as we please. Maybe there'll be other children here we can meet tomorrow. I expect some of the other evacuees are staying locally too".
"Maybe" replied Lawrence, still a little downcast and worried about making new acquaintances. "I do miss my mother and father though, don't you?"
"Yes" Rachel said. "I would rather be back at home, even if there were air raids every single night. But my parents wouldn't listen, not after what happened a few months ago."
"What happened?"
"Remember when lots of evacuees were sent back? Everyone thought there wouldn't be much of a war after all."
"Oh, yes. They called it the phoney war"
"Exactly. But then the bombs finally started. Some children in our street died the very next day when their house was hit. My mum and dad didn't want to send me away at all until then, but that did it."

Lawrence shuddered at the terrible loss of life that had already occurred.

“I knew some children who were killed that week too” he said sadly. He would never forget the feeling of going to school and seeing those empty desks. “I suppose we should think ourselves lucky to be here” he added reluctantly.

This sombre reminder of war subdued them once again, quelling their glimmer of optimism almost as soon as it had arrived. As the skies darkened and the trees stood as towering sentinels against the backdrop of the blood red sunset, Lawrence and Rachel retired regretfully inside to pass their first night in Burley.

Chapter 2

1990

Nick Rivers kicked his maths textbook onto the floor and flung himself onto his bed in anger.
"I don't *want* to go to the stupid New Forest!"

"What's all that noise in there?" called his father. "Have you finished that packing yet?"

Nick rolled his eyes to the heavens. "Nearly!" he shouted back, although really he had barely started. It wasn't fair, it just wasn't *fair*. All because he'd had that bout of bronchitis last year and his parents thought they should move away from London to a quieter place with fresher air. He thought people had stopped all this going away to the countryside for convalescence nonsense back in the Victorian era! He didn't want to leave his school, he didn't want to leave his friends, and he didn't want to leave the city he had grown up in. What was it his mum had said? "A quieter pace of life". Great. He was used to the hustle and bustle and couldn't imagine how people coped in little villages. How long would it take him to get anywhere worth going, for goodness' sake? He expected you had to hike ten miles to get to any decent shops, and he doubted there would be many teenagers his own age there. Would there even be any games arcades?

He had protested again and again, but his parents just wouldn't listen. Their patience had begun to wear thin and they warned him that he was being childish, and that at fourteen years old he should know better. They were going, and that was that. It was for his own good. They were going out of their way to improve things for the family and they would have to completely up sticks and find new jobs to do it, so he could damn well be a bit more grateful.

"Nick! If you don't finish packing your things by tomorrow morning, I'm throwing everything in the bin, and I mean it!" his mother's shrill call interrupted his thoughts.
"Alright, alright" he appeased her with an inward groan. "I'm doing it now".

He swung himself up into a seated position and surveyed his room and the balcony with the view across the city he loved so much, where he would stand for hours and watch the streams of people and traffic constantly moving like ants, day and night. He wouldn't have a view like this again – he enjoyed living here in the apartment high above the rest of the world, but now he would be stuck in a boring old house with nothing to see and nowhere to go.

He was being sent to the New Forest in two days when the school term finished, and was to stay in a village called Burley with Aunt Clarissa until his parents found new jobs and moved down permanently.

He had only met his aunt once or twice on her very rare visits to London but his memories of her were not promising; he recalled her as a rather eccentric woman in her early fifties with a penchant for garish outfits and what he deemed to be an excessive love of cats.

"Nicholas Rivers! This is the last time I'll warn you!" his mother stuck her head round the door, rustling a black bin bag with menace. He heaved a sigh and started to pack.

1990
Molly

My name's Molly and my mum's a witch. There – they're always telling us at school that you should begin a story with an attention-grabbing sentence. Well, it's not strictly the start of the story I suppose, as the scene has already been set, but it's the start of my part. Seeing as I'm the one making sure all this is recorded for posterity, we're going to do it my way. People complain that the stories I write are too confusing as I have a habit of switching from one perspective to another, but I'm sure you can keep up just fine. Too many people play an important part for it to be told from just one point of view. Writing's hard enough at the best of times, and you're likely to find yourself swimming in similes and messing about with metaphors so much that you forget the actual story you're meant to be telling. So if it's alright with you, I'll go ahead and tell it how I think best.

As I was saying. My mum's a witch, but that's not really unusual here. Oh, I'm not talking about the black cats and broomsticks nonsense and the witchcraft shops that draw in tourists, I mean the *real* witchcraft that goes on in the background here in the forest. The area has always been known for its myth and magic, and in the 1950s there was a famous white witch called Sybil Leek who strolled around with a jackdaw on her shoulder. Honestly, it's true. She wrote lots of books and eventually emigrated to America. But whatever you believe, it goes on. Don't jump to conclusions about cackling crones prancing around waving bats' blood; this isn't Macbeth you know. All I mean is that there are many people living here who would once have been misunderstood and hunted by the Witchfinder General, ultimately meeting an unpleasant end by hanging, drowning or being burnt at the stake. Some of them are Wiccans who worship the Goddess and carry out rituals; others simply practice their love of nature and use herbs in their daily lives. But they all have one thing in common which is respect for the earth, people and animals, and their one ultimate law is that they must not cause harm. Anyone who curses others or sends negative energy around is simply not a witch at all, and as far as this community is concerned, they would be an insult to the name.

But I'm getting ahead of myself again. Mum isn't really a practising witch and she only ever gathers with the others on the solstices each year, just for tradition, but she does a little herb work and she makes powerful salves and medicines for healing. She mostly keeps it quiet though, because there are people who still make assumptions and persecute others for their beliefs, even now in the 1990's.

My story started to get interesting on the first day of the summer holidays when I was woken by a kerfuffle early in the morning. I wondered if it was Miss Clutterbuck's cats next door fighting again, but I soon realised it was just a flurry of activity as a taxi had pulled up in her drive and she was greeting a teenage boy and taking a heavy looking suitcase from him before promptly fumbling with it and dropping it on his toe. I won't write down what he said about that.

Then the taxi drove away and she prodded him along into her house. I have to admit I was baffled, because she certainly doesn't have a son, and she rarely received visits from any relatives. I did vaguely remember some mention of a nephew in London, so perhaps this was him. I was quite curious because I didn't know what I was going to do with myself over the long summer break and the prospect of making a new friend was intriguing – I'm very chatty and enjoy spending time with people but a lot of the kids at school here think I'm weird, and they're probably right. My best friend Eliza is just like me and her parents are completely mad, but they had left that morning to go camping in a yurt in Mongolia so I didn't have anyone else to talk to.

I suspected the new arrival would come out of the house before long to get away from the lunacy inside (I've been into Miss Clutterbuck's home before, and the less said about that, the better), so I took a chair out to the front garden and loitered there reading a book for a while, waiting for him to emerge. Sure enough, he did.
"Hello!" I called out, giving a cheery wave. He ignored me as his eyes were glued to the games console he was holding. I was surprised he could walk along playing a game without tripping over.
"Hello?" I tried again. He looked up, startled, and promptly went flying, dropping his console on the ground. Oops.
I hurried over.
"Are you alright?" I asked.
"Oh, *I'm* fine" he said bitterly. "But my Atari Lynx! Look at it! The screen's cracked."

"Oh. Sorry" I said, although I didn't think it was *really* my fault. I did call out and distract him, but he was the one not paying attention to where he was going.
"Anyway, I'm Molly. Are you Miss Clutterbuck's nephew?"
He scowled and looked as if he might not reply.
"Yes, unfortunately" he said eventually, giving me a look of annoyance. He told me his name was Nick and he had been sent here from London against his will to live in the New Forest, but while his parents organised their house and new jobs, he was staying with his aunt over the summer. It turned out he was 15, just a few months older than me and would be starting at the same school in September.
"Anyway" he said. "It's a madhouse in there with my aunt. I've been attacked by three of her cats and fallen over a trifle already".
"Sounds like you're a bit clumsy then!"

I meant it as a joke, but it was obviously a *big* mistake. He looked back at his cracked Atari Puma or whatever-on-earth it is and then looked back at me with anger in his eyes.
"It's your fault" he growled. "If you hadn't been sitting there waving at me like an idiot, I wouldn't have tripped. What am I going to do without it, here at the back of beyond? There's *nothing* to do!"
"Nothing to do? There's plenty"
"Plenty? Ha. Well, you enjoy your pathetic little trees and horses. I don't want anything to do with it."

He stormed back into Miss Clutterbuck's house and slammed the front door. I rolled my eyes. That was the end of that, then. I went back inside, not really wanting to admit my disappointment at the lost opportunity to make a new friend. I consoled myself with thinking about how irritating he probably would have been anyway – he obviously didn't want to be here, and I could only imagine how he would react if he found out my mum is a witch. Besides, his sweatshirt could have done with a good wash and he had a habit of flicking his stupid, floppy hair out of his eyes every five seconds. I amused myself with imagining him landing face first in Miss Clutterbuck's trifle, and spent the rest of the morning quietly reading.

The following day, I was cabin feverish and couldn't stay at home a moment longer without getting a breath of fresh air, so I decided to take my camera down to Mill Lawn. There used to be a watermill there which stopped running in about 1820, and the only surviving building is the grist house in the grounds of Mill Cottage. I want to study photography at college as I love taking pictures, and I thought I might be able to capture some atmospheric shots. I once wanted to be a writer, but as I said, drowning in diphthongs and grappling with gerunds can really take the fun out of things.

So, imagine my surprise and annoyance when I bumped into you-know-who in the shop where I dropped in to pick up some new film on my way.
"Oh, it's you" I said drably.
"Oh, it's *you*" he said back, not very originally.
He browsed the crisps while I stood in the queue to pay for my roll of film.

“What’ve you got there then?” he asked, following me as I left the shop and peering at my camera in what I thought was a very nosey manner.
“It’s my camera” I said slowly, as though talking to an idiot.
“I know *that*” he replied. “I mean, what are you up to with it? Wouldn’t have thought there’s much to take pictures of round here”

After yesterday, I wasn’t surprised at his opinion that the miles and miles of scenery, fields full of horses and donkeys, chocolate-box cottages and forests of trees were not worth photographing but it made me bristle anyway. I raised both eyebrows, not having yet perfected the art of an appropriately condescending single-eyebrow sneer, and gave him what I hoped was a withering stare.
“Well” I said. “It’s all a lot more interesting than pictures of red double-decker buses and dirty streets.”

“Alright, don’t get huffy. I’m sorry” he replied, and I nearly fell over in surprise at his apology, half-baked though it was. “I didn’t mean to be rude yesterday.” He scuffed the ground with the toe of his trainer and looked embarrassed.
“It’s okay. And I’m sorry I made you drop your Atari Jaguar”
“Atari Lynx” he corrected me with a snigger.
“Whatever. Anyway, I *am* sorry. I’d be angry too if there were pages ripped out of my favourite book or something, if I didn’t have anything else to do”.
“It’s fine” he shrugged. “Well, not really. But it’s kind of old now. I want to get the Gameboy when it comes out in September anyway. I just…didn’t want

to come here in the first place. I've only been in there with Aunt Clarissa for a day and it's driving me mad. If she plays that harp at two o'clock in the morning again –"

I couldn't refrain from laughing and his eyes lit up with a tiny spark of something I hadn't seen in him yesterday – a sense of humour. There was obviously one in there somewhere. I supposed I would have been bad tempered too in his position, but I wasn't quite willing to let him off the hook so soon.

"So, you never said where you're off to for taking photos" he reminded me. I sighed, unwilling to tell anyone about the quiet, interesting old places I love to visit.
"Just the site of the old mill" I told him reluctantly as I started to walk.
"So what about it?" he said, keeping pace with me.
"What about what?"
"Can I come with you? Will you show me this old place you want to take pictures of?"
"I don't think you'd find it very interesting"
"No, I doubt it" he admitted. "But as there's not even a cinema or shopping centre for miles, I haven't got any other options. Especially as I can't even play games now".

I sighed, knowing I had no choice. I had been partly to blame for the breakage, after all. To be honest, I didn't *really* mind the suggestion – although I like peace and quiet while I'm walking and taking pictures, it's not often that I shut up (or so people tell me), and having some company *would* be nice. But

of course I didn't want to let him know that, so I pretended to think about it for a moment.
"Oh, all right then" I agreed grudgingly. "As long as you promise to let me concentrate, and not to say anything else for the rest of the day about how much you hate it here."
He flipped his hair out of his eyes again in that infuriating gesture of his.
"Okay, promise"

Chapter 3

1940

"Wake up! We're missing all the excitement!"
Lawrence blearily opened his eyes to find Rachel shaking his arm.
"What are you doing in my room?" he mumbled.
"Something's happening. Look out of the window" she gestured. "I heard noises and saw a crowd of people walking past, carrying all sorts of odd things like brooms and sprigs of holly. Get up! D'you see them?"

Lawrence stumbled groggily to the window, drawing back the blackout curtains and staring out into the darkness in vain.
"No, I don't see anything. Are you sure you didn't dream it?"
Rachel sighed theatrically.
"Of course I'm sure, because I was awake. I can't sleep very well here."
She pushed him out of the way and looked out of the window again herself.
"They're gone" she admitted. "If you'd woken up more quickly you might've seen them. Oh, wait! I thought I just saw a movement over there." She pointed towards a thicket of trees barely visible in the pale light of the crescent moon. "Yes, they've definitely gone into the trees. What could they be up to?"

Lawrence turned to get back into bed.

"I don't know and don't care. I'm going back to sleep".

The two of them had been slowly settling into a routine at Mrs Fernley's for the last few days. They had taken to helping her with the breakfast and dinner preparations each day which served to put her in a slightly better mood, and while she was at work they roamed around the village and walked for miles just stretching their legs and enjoying the sunshine; there was little else to do so they had to invent their own amusements. They had been disappointed to discover that most of the other evacuees had travelled further on to other small forest villages and there didn't seem to be many other young people around. They had each written to their parents to assure them of their safe arrival, but they had no other contact with the outside world and were still getting accustomed to their new lifestyle which was particularly hard for the quiet, homely Lawrence who had never been away from his parents before – although it seemed he had no difficulties in falling asleep at night.
Rachel tugged at his pyjama sleeve. "Come on grumpy, don't go back to sleep! Get dressed; we're going to see what's going on."
"Oh for goodness sake, you're beginning to sound like Nancy Drew the Detective" Lawrence sighed, irked by the insistence of his companion.
"I don't think it's a good idea" he added, knowing that his protestations would probably be ignored but feeling he ought to try anyway, "What if it's something to do with the war? It could be a German invasion. Perhaps we should wake Mrs Fernley and ask her to telephone the authorities?"

But the words sounded weak even to his own ears, so at Rachel's urging he donned a jacket over his pyjamas and laced up his outdoor shoes.
"We'll need torches though" he reminded her, realising that if they were to embark on such a hare-brained adventure, they had better be fully prepared and avoid tripping over tree stumps and breaking their necks.

A few minutes later they were hurrying towards the dark cluster of trees, shining the torchlight from side to side and up and down, trying to make out where the mysterious group had gone.
Rachel jumped as Lawrence stepped on a branch with a sharp snap.
"Ssh! Keep quiet you idiot!" she elbowed him.
"Alright, alright" he whispered, growing more concerned by the minute. He still missed home terribly, but his sadness had been partly replaced with irritation, and he lamented his bad luck at being dragged into an escapade like this by the persistent Rachel. It wasn't pitch black as the moon was giving off a little light but wisps of cloud drifted across it, momentarily casting them into deeper darkness before the scene was bathed in the gentle white glow once more. In the moments when the moonlight shone through the clouds, they were able to pick their way more rapidly into the woods, keeping a close eye on the ground so as not to lose their footing.
"I hope there aren't any snakes here" Lawrence whispered.
Rachel shuddered.

Then they heard voices.

It was cool for a summer evening, but they were both fairly sure it wasn't just the breeze making their hair stand on end and chills run up and down their spines. They stopped in their tracks and listened carefully. There was a voice – no, *many* voices, whispering and murmuring indecipherably, the volume rising and rising and the speed increasing in frenzy. They weren't sure where the sound was coming from, but it couldn't be far away. They strained their ears to pick out any words they could recognise, but it sounded almost like a different language.
"D'you think it's German?" Rachel hissed. "It's definitely not English. Maybe you're right. Could they be spies after all?"
It was Lawrence's turn to nudge her with impatience. "No, of course it's not. Don't you know what German sounds like? And keep your voice low."

After a few moments of indecision, they continued their slow creep forward through the trees. Lawrence was certainly not convinced that it was a sensible idea, but since they had come so far, their curiosity had to be satisfied. They couldn't turn back now. Slowly, slowly they picked their way across the forest floor until the trees started to thin, and the voices became louder and clearer.
To avoid being detected now they were closer, they switched off the torch and were plunged into almost complete blackness. Gripping onto each other to avoid losing their footing, they gradually fumbled their way to the edge of the thicket.
"Look!" Rachel pointed.

They could see flickering light. As their eyes adjusted, they nearly gasped aloud as they made out a glade filled with people, joining hands in a circle around a fire. One of them stood in the centre and appeared to be sweeping the ground vigorously with a broom. Another was dancing around the outside of the circle scattering something from a pot. Their shapes were indistinct and hard to make out, but it looked like they were dressed in long, sweeping robes.
The murmuring voices fell silent and the figure holding the broom began half-singing, half-intoning some strange words in a strong, resonant soprano. A frisson seemed to run through the group. Lawrence and Rachel shivered at the odd change in the atmosphere, the air charged as if before an electrical storm. The voice was rising to a crescendo and the other members of the group resumed their low murmuring once more, creating an eerie symphony.

Suddenly, there was a scream. The chanting stopped and the fire was extinguished in a chill gust of wind. There was a moment of silence, and then all hell broke loose. More screaming, shouting, crying. People thundered backwards and forwards, throwing the woods into chaos. Even though the scene was no longer visible in the sudden darkness, it was obvious that panic permeated the air.

And then they both felt it. A dark, forbidding wave cascaded over them, filling them with inexplicable terror and the sense that they had to – they *must* - escape.

They couldn't see what was happening, but surer than anything they had ever felt in their lives, they knew with the utmost certainty that they were in danger. Throwing caution to the winds, they turned on their heels and sprinted through the forest. Their breath came in ragged pants as they ran, stumbling through the undergrowth. Low branches whipped Rachel's bare legs as they raced with abandon. Lawrence held his hands in front of his face to protect it from head-height boughs, but lost his footing and nearly fell. Rachel grabbed his arm and pulled him steady.

Hearts pounding like drums, they clung to each other as they ran, not daring to look back, feeling that intense, dark presence behind them as if in pursuit. They knew, they just *knew* that if they stopped, they would be caught by something dreadful, something demonic, something wordlessly evil.
As they ran, Lawrence nearly screamed as he saw a pair of green eyes glinting in the darkness. His stomach constricted and a shiver ran up and down his spine. There was a sudden rustle above them. And then they heard it. A terrible, chilling, moaning cry. They couldn't look up, keeping their eyes to the ground as they desperately tried to escape. It sounded like someone or some*thing* moving in the trees overhead.

When they broke through the forest and emerged into the road to see Mrs Fernley's cottage so reassuringly waiting for them, they were flooded with the greatest relief they had ever experienced.

As they put more and more distance between themselves and the woods, they felt the pressure lift and the wave of panic dissipated as quickly as it had come. They stopped running and doubled over, hands on knees, panting and gasping, only now noticing their burning lungs and shaking legs.

They couldn't speak. They looked back towards the cluster of trees and saw nothing to indicate that anything at all had happened. The whole experience seemed unreal now that the terrifying feeling of oppressive darkness had left them, and they could no longer hear any unusual sounds, not even the crack of a twig.

Once they had caught their breath, they quickly and quietly retreated inside the cottage and straight to bed, fervently hoping that Mrs Fernley remained asleep and unaware of their nocturnal adventure. They both lay in their rooms staring up at the ceiling, and stayed there for the rest of the night in uneasy wakefulness until the dawn broke.

Rachel and Lawrence's eyes met over their eggs and toast the next morning, and they waited with impatience for Mrs Fernley to leave for work so they could discuss the night's events. They were fractious and tired from lack of sleep, and Lawrence fumbled with his fork and dropped it on the floor with a clatter.

"Sorry Mrs Fernley" he mumbled, bending down to retrieve it. He couldn't help but see that Rachel's legs were covered with scratches from yesterday's flight through the forest, and he hoped they wouldn't be noticed.

"I don't know what's got into you two this morning" their unwilling hostess replied tartly. "You seem on edge and you look very tired. I warn you, if you're up to something I shall find out."
"We're finding it difficult to sleep here sometimes" Rachel came to the rescue. "We're still a bit homesick. We're used to the noise of the town you see, so it seems strange to us that it's so quiet here at night".
Mrs Fernley narrowed her eyes at them.
"Well, just you mind that you stay out of trouble" she sniffed. "But you'll be pleased to hear that you've each received a letter this morning – no doubt they're from home".
Their spirits soared at the thought of news from their families, and distracted momentarily from last night's horrors, they ripped open the envelopes once they were safely alone and greedily devoured the news.
Lawrence's read;

"Our dearest Lawrence,
Thank you for your letter which we were delighted to receive; we are easier in our minds now we know you have arrived safely and are staying in such a beautiful part of the country away from the bombing. We hope you are well and now nicely settled into your billet, and we are happy to know that you are not the only evacuee there. Having a friend always helps during times of upheaval.

I am thankful that your father's leg trouble prevents him from being called up, but he is as proud as a peacock to have been accepted into the Home Guard. He was on fire-watching duty for the first time last night and feels satisfied that he is now making a contribution to the war effort.

I have also started working in the munitions factory. Now that we needn't worry about looking after you, Lawrence, we can both do our bit for the war effort whilst knowing you are safe in Burley. The work is not too tiring so far, but I have only been there a couple of days and am still being trained. As you know, it is only a ten minute walk from our house so I do not have to worry about buses not running; Mrs Green's girl Valerie next door has a terribly long journey to her work in the milliner's shop. It's alright now it's summertime but I'm sure you remember she had some real scrapes in the winter when she had to find her way home in the blackout. There was an air raid last night but thankfully nothing in these streets was hit, but we heard that the dockyard was badly damaged.

I must end this now by saying that your father and I both miss you awfully, but hope you are enjoying your holiday in the country! Do write again soon, and please convey our grateful thanks to your Mrs Fernley for looking after you for us.
With love,
Mother
P.S. I enclose a postal order for five shillings – do stretch it out if you can!"

Lawrence smiled weakly as he finished the letter, happy to hear from them but anxious for their safety. Who knew when and where a bomb would fall next? Those children from school haunted his thoughts;

smiling and laughing one moment and then gone the next. That could happen to his parents.

There was a tap on the door and Rachel stuck her head in.
"Have you finished yours?" she didn't bother to hide her curiosity.
"Yes, have you?"
"Yes, and I've been sent a five shilling postal order!"
"Ha, me too!"
"So we've ten shillings between us if we club together. That's an awful lot; just think what we could get with that."
"Not half as much as we'd like, seeing as sweets are rationed now" Lawrence reminded her.
"What did yours say then?" asked Rachel.
"Oh, nothing much" he shrugged. "Yours?"
"Me neither" she replied cagily, tucking her long black hair behind her ears.

Neither were willing to elaborate, wanting to keep their 'old' lives secret in some measure, perhaps subconsciously distancing themselves from it as a coping mechanism.

Here and now, they were living in Burley as evacuees, far from home, family and friends, and adapting to that was what mattered for the moment. They both missed their parents more than they expressed, and Rachel didn't want Lawrence to know how much the contents of her letter had affected her. It had read;

"Dear Rachel,
This is a brief letter for now I'm afraid. I have had to move in with your Aunt Betty to help take care of things in the house, as she has just received the sad news that your Uncle Harold was killed in a naval battle in Norway in April; it has taken this long to send telegrams to inform the families of all involved.

He died bravely in the fighting between the British Navy and the Nazi's Kriegsmarine. He needn't have gone, being above the conscription age, but you know how eager he was to do his duty. He'd been a soldier for so long it was in his blood and he simply couldn't do anything else. I know you were fond of him. I am helping to look after your cousins for a short while until your Aunt feels better, but I don't know how they'll all cope in the future.

Your father and I live in fear of his being conscripted eventually. He is a pacifist as you know, but he was insulted in the street yesterday by a group of soldiers who jeered at him, saying he should volunteer if he's fit and able.
I fear a white feather is on its way sooner or later, and I am saddened that this sort of thing is a regular occurrence for those whose conscience will not allow them to fight.

We are happy you have safely reached your new home. Remember to always mind your manners and listen to this Mrs Fernley and behave well for her. Many other children are not so fortunate; I'm very sorry to tell you that Jemima Brown was killed in an air raid this week; some of the streets near the

dockyard were almost flattened. I think she was in your class at school and understand she was too unwell to travel with the other evacuees and was to be sent away as soon as she had got over the whooping cough. It makes us feel better to know you are out of harm's way. I'm putting in a postal order for five shillings.
Love from Mum (and Dad)

Rachel was very upset to hear of Uncle Harold's death. Although he hadn't been able to visit very often, he had been such a character that the few memories she did have of him were bright and vivid.

Tall and broad with a crinkly smile, he told wonderful stories of his adventures in the army and the places he'd seen, and she'd been fascinated by the way his salt-and-pepper moustache bobbed up and down as he laughed.
He'd been stationed in India for a while and one of her favourite tales had been about when he was on cooking duty one hot, sultry afternoon. A huge tiger had come out of nowhere and wandered into the kitchen. Harold could see the strength of its muscles and sinews rippling under its dusty orange and black coat.

He had clutched his ladle like a weapon, ignoring the drips of stew which plinked onto the stone floor as he held his breath. The tiger had stalked up and down, a dull thrum reverberating from its throat. Harold could do nothing but stand perfectly still. Eventually it had settled down on the floor just inches from his feet, and fallen fast asleep.

Rachel remembered giggling, tugging at her uncle's sleeve and asking, "What happened next, what happened next?" even though she had heard it many times before.

"I stood there for an hour" he would answer, lighting a cigar. "Waiting until I was quite sure the blighter was snoozing. To this day, I don't know where all the other fellows had gone, but I was quite alone. Nobody came, although it's just as well they didn't; they'd have walked straight into the brute unawares. In the end, I had to summon the courage to tiptoe around him and then ran like the dickens. I found the other chaps and we went back there carefully, armed with guns in case things got sticky. Of course, the tiger was gone, and not one of them believed me!"

Rachel smiled sadly at the memory. She didn't want to talk about it, so she covered up her feelings with bravado, refusing to let Lawrence see any vulnerability. That was how she coped. She noticed that Lawrence became sulky or grumpy when he was upset, and she understood that. She was usually vivacious and cheerful and didn't often feel down in the dumps, but when she did, pretending to be as happy as usual seemed to help a bit. Besides, with the war on, everyone seemed to have bigger problems to worry about. Nobody appeared to be particularly concerned about evacuated children missing their homes; after all, they were lucky to be away from danger. Everyone talked about having a 'stiff upper lip' and of course there were many others far worse off, so she supposed they had to grin and bear it.

What both Rachel and Lawrence struggled to grasp was the speed at which things could change. Less than a week had passed since they had left home, but in that time so much had happened. Lawrence's father had joined the Home Guard and his mother had started work in a munitions factory. Rachel's aunt had received tragic news and her father had been ridiculed in the street. Most harrowing of all, a girl of their own age was dead and would never again write compositions in the classroom, sing hymns in morning assembly or fill the playground with laughter.

Shaking off these unhappy thoughts, their attention turned once more to the previous night. They both wanted to discuss it, but neither quite knew how to start putting it into words. They decided to walk to the village post office to make good on their postal orders but felt a little subdued.
"What do you think it was?" Rachel eventually broached the subject.
Lawrence was troubled, frowning until his eyebrows met. He had been hoping that it was just a bad dream but hearing Rachel give voice to their experience made him realise with finality that it wasn't.
"I don't know" he replied. "But I don't like it. Who were those people, and what where they doing? It looked like some kind of ritual."
"Witchcraft" stated Rachel.
"What, in 1940?" countered Lawrence. "That sort of thing doesn't go on any more. Perhaps it was some sort of secret war meeting."

"What, all dressed in robes and chanting?" Rachel scoffed. "And what would they be doing with brooms and sprigs of holly?"
Lawrence had to admit she had a point.
"D'you think it's possible then?" he asked, feeling silly. "Could there really still be people who play at witchcraft?"
"Not *play* at witchcraft!" Rachel corrected him. "That wasn't some sort of game. Whatever it was, it was real. And what about those eyes in the darkness? And the cries we heard?"

Lawrence didn't have a chance to reply. As the children neared the Post Office, they came across a gaggle of elderly women clustered outside. Two of them were in tears and the whole group was noticeably flustered and distressed.
"What's going on?" Lawrence turned to Rachel.
One of the women overheard him.
"The post office will be closed today" she said, wiping away a tear. "Haven't you heard? Margery Blackthorn, the lady who runs it, was found…" she faltered, "found dead in the woods this morning."
The sound of authoritative voices made them spin round.
"Out of the way, out of the way, ladies! No blocking the road, please".
Two policemen were carrying a stretcher along the lane, presumably towards the doctor's office. To the children's horror, there was a motionless shape on top, entirely covered by a large white sheet.

“What happened?” Rachel’s voice trembled as the sombre parade passed by, unable to avert her eyes from the horribly compelling sight.
“Nobody knows. They think perhaps she had a heart attack but her face was twisted in the most *awful* way, as if in terrible fear.”
“Lucy, you mustn’t tell the children such things!” one of the other ladies chided her. “It will give them nightmares.”

They knew they would learn nothing more, so they wordlessly turned and headed back to the cottage, their postal orders temporarily forgotten. Neither of them spoke any more that day about the fate of Margery Blackthorn or the wave of terror they had felt last night that made them flee for their lives, but it was never far from their thoughts. Overwhelmed by the horrifying discovery and unable to comprehend how the events they had witnessed were connected, the silence between them weighed heavy.

Chapter 4

1990

After calling their reluctant truce, Nick and Molly strolled to the site of the old mill. Nick found the place unimpressive and couldn't understand Molly's enthusiasm. They couldn't get very close to the original site of the mill because all that remained of the grist house was in the grounds of somebody's cottage, but she knew all the hidden recesses between the trees which allowed her to snap some peaceful scenes in the half-shade provided by the sunlight-dappled leaves.

She clambered onto a low brick wall and gestured for Nick to join her.

"Look, do you see that waterfall?" she called. "It's in somebody's garden now but that's where the original mill wheel was."

Nick shrugged.

"It's cool, I guess" he said, trying his best to be polite after their earlier disagreement.

Molly shifted into a sitting position on the wall, swinging her legs.

"I know you're bored" she said equably. "I've taken my pictures now, so what do you want to do?" She wasn't quite sure yet whether Nick would become a friend, or merely someone to tolerate, but her open and friendly nature took over – after all, she reasoned to herself, she knew how it felt to be 'the odd one out' and sensed that he was feeling very out of sorts in a place so different from what he was used to.

"Well, what is there to do?" he asked doubtfully.
"Horse riding, cycling, walking, the witchcraft shops…" Nick's look of distaste stopped her short. "…or you can come over and we can just listen to music or something".
"Ah, now that sounds more like my sort of thing" he grinned. "Safely inside away from all that country air!"
"We'll make a country bumpkin of you yet" Molly joked.
Back at home when she led him up a set of rickety, wooden spiral stairs to what can only be described as an Aladdin's Cave, he was astonished.
"What's this?" he asked, baffled. "It's not your bedroom is it?"
Molly laughed, her green eyes sparkling. "No, my bedroom is downstairs. This is what I call the Nook. It's not all *my* stuff. Some of it is my mum's and most of it has been here as long as I can remember. Probably my gran's too – she used to own the house."

The attic room was crammed with trinkets and ornaments, crooked bookshelves and boxes of papers. Nick had to stoop to avoid hitting his head on the sloping eaves, and promptly walked into a model witch on a broomstick dangling dangerously from the ceiling.

"I'm beginning to think this is as bad as my aunt's house next door" he muttered, and Molly suddenly wondered whether it was a good idea to bring him here.
Her eyes flicked around quickly as she tried to remember if there was anything obvious on display

that might give away her mum's interest in witchcraft, which she was quite sure Nick wouldn't understand. The dangling witch could be written off as a bit of fun, but herbs and athames might be harder to explain.

To distract him, she pulled up two beanbag chairs from the corner and invited him to sit down, brushing aside a couple of candles and a black receptacle that to the uninitiated might look suspiciously like a cauldron.

"What kinda music do you like? Judging by that grungy old sweatshirt you wear, I'm going to guess Nirvana."
Nick chuckled and flipped his hair out of his eyes in his ever-present gesture. "Right. But you look more like a Joan Jett type yourself"
"Well, we *are* perceptive today, aren't we? Anyway, I have tapes of both. What do you fancy?"

Nick occupied himself in inspecting the room with its eclectic furnishings and geegaws, noticing a stained-glass Yin and Yang symbol in the window and multiple plastic moons and stars stuck to the ceiling. The scent in the air was hard to describe, but it was an old, musty smell in a *good* way, like the aroma of a rediscovered favourite childhood book that had been hiding on a long-forgotten shelf for years. It was a strange room, but it felt cosy. In fact, everything about Molly and her home felt very cosy and natural somehow, and she had been friendly and accepting to him as a newcomer despite his bad humour at being there and the fact he had been rude yesterday when they had first met in the garden. He was still annoyed about his Atari Lynx, but he felt a little guilty for his derision of Burley and thought he should ask Molly about the history of the area, as he suspected she'd welcome the opportunity to talk about it – and besides, it *might* be interesting. After all, he was stuck here whether he liked it or not, so he might as well try to make the best of it and cultivate his only possible friendship in this place.

"There are lots of stories" she was enthusiastic when he asked. "We've got ghosts, smugglers, a dragon, witches…"
"How about the smugglers?" Nick's interest was piqued. "What did they smuggle?"

"Anything really, but usually it was tea, coffee, salt, spirits – things they should have been paying taxes on. They came from the coast and used paths across the forests and moors to transport it. Some builders recently found a secret chamber underneath the Stable Bar in The Queen's Head pub in the village, where smugglers had stashed their gold coins and pistols and bottles hundreds of years ago. They were probably trying to hide them from the government, but nobody knows why they never came back for them later. Maybe it was too dangerous if the place was being watched, and they just cut their losses and moved on."

Molly was warming to her story.
"There's a local legend that a gang came to Burley to rest overnight, bring their booty with them, because

the Queen's Head was a popular hideout for smugglers and highwaymen. They were betrayed, and the revenue men rode up in the night and surprised them. One of their sisters had discovered the danger they were in, and rushed out into the storm, racing against time to reach the inn and warn her brother Jeremiah and his gang before they were caught."

"So what happened? Did they escape?" Nick interrupted.

"You'll find out if you keep quiet and listen" Molly nudged him. "As I was saying. Almost all the men were able to escape, and Jeremiah sacrificed himself by distracting the excise men, as they called them in those days, giving his gang precious time to creep away. He was taken to jail and nobody knows what happened to him after that, but the conditions were usually so terrible that if he wasn't hung, he most likely died in there anyway. There are lots of well-known smuggling families in the area. One of them was called Warne and they lived on Crow-Hill Top. Their sister would put on a red cloak and walk across the hills if she knew the revenue men were around, as a sign to other smugglers at a distance coming from the coast. Sometimes they would hang a lantern in an oak tree as a signal."

Nick was becoming increasingly curious.
"You talk about it like it's a good thing the smugglers got away. But they were criminals, right?"
"Depends which way you look at it" Molly replied thoughtfully. "Really, the reason so many did it was the high taxes. The government were always

demanding more money to pay for the wars they wanted to join so ordinary people and businesses suffered. If they hadn't smuggled some of their goods in to avoid paying the levies, they might have starved."

"What wars were going on at that time, then?" interjected Nick.

"They were always fighting about something or other," Molly sighed at the interruption. "But the American Revolution was around that time and went on for years. Anyway, the ones who did it just to make a profit were the real criminals, and the violent ones who killed the government men who chased them. Some of them even murdered members of their own gangs in disputes."

"Hmm" Nick said. "It's quite interesting, actually"
"Anyway" Molly continued. "Apparently the ghost of Jeremiah the heroic smuggler still roams the area to this day"
"Wooooo, scary" Nick mocked, waving his arms as if to imitate a phantom.
Molly gave him a look.
"Alright, don't come running to me screaming when you see him" she said.
"I doubt that will happen, somehow"
"Don't be so sure"
"Have you seen him then?"
"No, but that's not the point. Lots of people have".

Nick was unconvinced and they were both silent for a moment before Molly piped up again,

“Hey, I just remembered a picture I painted when I was little. I loved everything to do with smugglers and mysteries and I was always drawing them – I won a prize for this one. I wonder if it’s still up here.” She navigated her way across the cluttered loft and rummaged through a mismatched mahogany dresser in the corner of the room.
“Here we are!” she was triumphant within moments. Nick wondered how she could possibly find something so quickly amongst all the clutter. He stood up to make his way over to take a look, but stumbled on a loose floorboard and fell headlong on the floor, putting a hand out to break his fall and knocking several boxes off a nearby table with a thud. Papers and books were scattered and they both coughed as a cloud of dust rose up.
“Oh god, I’m sorry” Nick groaned, pulling himself up and dusting off his jeans. “I hope I haven’t broken anything”
“Don’t worry” Molly waved her hand dismissively. “It’s only papers, and it’s a tip up here anyway; I’ll pick it all up.”
“I meant I hope *I* haven’t broken anything!” Nick retorted, rubbing his bruised knee with a grimace of pain.
Molly smiled mischievously. “That’s twice – no, three times you’ve fallen over in two days now. I hope you didn’t make this much mess when you tripped over Miss Clutterbuck’s trifle”
“Very funny. Let me help, then” he grumbled, picking up stacks of yellowing papers and placing them neatly back in their boxes.
“What’s this?” he asked after a moment. “The rest just looks like bills and paperwork but this is

someone's diary."

The painting forgotten, Molly shuffled through the chaos and carefully inspected Nick's find. It was rather dog-eared, yellowing and crinkled, with a smell reminiscent of old, dusty museums. The word 'Diary' on the front was a giveaway, but it was only when she opened the front cover that she found the handwriting inside, a little faded but still legible. It read,

"This is the diary of Rachel Morgan, 1940, aged 12. TOP SECRET! Do not read. (Yes, that means you, Lawrence)".

1990
Molly

When Nick knocked those boxes over, I must admit my first thought (after rolling my eyes at how clumsy he was), was that there might be witch stuff in there like Books of Shadows or charms, so I tried to be casual so as not to arouse his interest too much but secretly hoped he wouldn't see anything incriminating. What he did find though, was completely unexpected to both of us. And living in this place, I've learnt to expect the unexpected.

When I saw the writing inside the diary and read the name Rachel Morgan, I knew straight away it must have been my gran's. We've lived here with her for as long as I can remember, and she grew up here too. When she died, the house was officially passed down to my mum. Unusually, she had kept her maiden name when she got married and so did mum, so that's why we're all Morgans. They were always talking about the suffragettes and how lucky I am to have been born in an era of equal rights, and mum is quite the feminist which is why she kept her name when she and dad got married.

Dad is often abroad on business by the way, which is why he hasn't appeared in the story. He's just as mad as the rest of us in his own way, and spends most of his time travelling to unusual places searching for valuable antiques – but that deserves a whole story of its own.

Anyway, I didn't know a lot about my gran and I was quite young when she died. Some of my memories of her are as a secretive and quiet woman who didn't talk about herself much, yet she was always happy to chat to me for hours about even the silliest things I could imagine in my rampant childhood imagination. Her emerald eyes always held a spark, and there was a quirk of a smile that twitched the corners of her lips as though she had once been a lot livelier. But when she was tired, which was often as she became very ill towards the end, you could read between the lines of her face and know that she'd seen a lot in her life. She didn't knit like other grannies, instead she read a lot of books and she *thought*. She was quite happy sitting for hours lost in goodness-knows-what, although she joked that when she was younger she couldn't keep quiet for a moment.

"You take after me, Molly" she'd said with a wink. But that was one of the only times she had ever mentioned her youth. As far as I was concerned, she had always been old.

All I really knew from mum was that gran had originally lived in Portsmouth but had been evacuated here to Burley during World War II. I didn't know why she stayed, or whether she did return home when the war was over, and simply chose to come back and settle here later as an adult. I'm not sure even my mum knew.

So holding this diary sent a magical little tingle through my fingers as I realised this would give me a unique insight into what her life had been like when she was sent here during the war. I couldn't believe I'd never known it was there, but then I'd had no reason to imagine it would be. I wondered how she felt when she had been evacuated, and who 'Lawrence' was.

To give him credit, Nick was very polite about the whole thing.
"If you want to read it alone, I understand" he said, flicking his hair out of his eyes again.
He was obviously curious though, to my surprise.
"I didn't think you were interested in stuff like this anyway".
"I guess not" he replied, "but it's either that or go back next door and get attacked by my aunt's seven cats again."
I raised my eyes to the heavens. I should have known. Of course he wasn't really interested in the history; he just didn't have anything better to do.

I turned Nirvana down to a background murmur and we sat cross-legged on the attic floor and started to read.

Chapter 5

1940

"What d'you think we should do?" Rachel broke the silence the day after the terrible news that the Post Office lady had been found dead.
"What do you mean, *do?* What *can* we do?" Lawrence frowned irritably.
"About Margery Blackthorn" Rachel explained impatiently. "She was found dead in the woods the morning after we went there! We're witnesses. We saw what happened, perhaps we should tell the police."
"Tell the police? Do you really think they'd believe we saw some kind of witchcraft ritual going on in the middle of the night?"
Rachel scowled back at him.
"Well, they should. Because it's true, we *did* see it. It must have something to do with Margery's death. They said she had a look of terror on her face. What else could have caused that? Don't tell me you've forgotten how scared we were when we felt that… darkness come down over us."

It was the first time either of them had described the feeling they had experienced when their panic and terror had driven them to flee madly from the forest as if pursued by the devil himself.
Lawrence looked uneasy.
"No, of course I haven't" he admitted. "It was horrifying. The worst thing I've ever felt, and just mentioning it makes me shiver.

But neither the police, nor anyone else is going to believe it and there's no evidence. If we say anything at all about being there that night, it will make us look suspicious."

"But there *might* be some evidence" Rachel said, tapping her cheek thoughtfully with a finger, the nail bitten down to the quick. "There'd be some remains from the fire, wouldn't there? And we saw them scattering something on the ground, so there might still be a trace of whatever that was. Why don't we go and have a look today while it's light? If we find anything we'll tell the police. Then they'll have to come and investigate, and they'll see we're not lying".

Lawrence couldn't suppress a shudder at the thought of returning to the forest.
"I don't know" he hesitated. "Whoever or *whatever* killed Margery might be still be there. Besides, if there was anything to find, the police would already have found it, wouldn't they?"

Rachel had to accept that this was true. People didn't drop dead in the woods without the police conducting a full investigation.
"Well, there's no harm in looking anyway, is there?" she persisted. "The police are always busy, especially now with the war on, and so many have left to join the forces. They could have missed something".

Lawrence was reluctant but held up his hands in appeasement.

“Alright” he yielded wearily. “But on the condition that if we don’t find anything, we agree to keep quiet. There’s no good in making ourselves look ridiculous and having the police tell Mrs Fernley what we’ve been up to. I don’t know what my parents would say if she threw us out on our ear”. He held back his sadness as he mentioned his parents, growing slowly more accustomed to life as an evacuee. He still wished he had his sketchbook, though. He would far rather sit drawing for hours than go running around in the woods looking for trouble, and Rachel’s constant energy made him feel tired.

They wasted no further time in making their way back to the scene of the terror they had witnessed two nights before, but they hadn’t walked far before they spotted a constable standing guard near a patch of scrubby grass, hands clasped behind his back and chest puffed out with importance.
“Ssh!” Rachel warned Lawrence, pushing him behind an oak tree and sidling behind it with him. “I don’t think he’s seen us”.
“Who’s there?” the police officer whipped round and scanned the foliage, suspicion on his face.
They held their breath and waited, trying to make themselves as small as possible behind the tree. The constable stood still and attentive, listening out for further movement, but as luck would have it, he wasn’t facing in their direction.

Moments later, crunching twigs and rustling leaves alerted them to someone else’s approach.
“Who’s there, I say? Identify yourself!” the constable snapped officiously.

"It's me, you fool. Inspector Bagthorpe from the Yard. You're Peterson I presume? I hope you realise I've been called away from a Lord Taverners match for this!"

"They've sent someone from Scotland Yard!" Lawrence breathed. Rachel peered very carefully around the tree and saw that the Inspector was dressed head to toe in cricket whites and was swinging his bat around in a rather haphazard manner.

"Sorry about that, sir" Constable Peterson said. "Sorry! Well I should think so. 49 runs not out, about to get my first half century of the season and some imbecile comes running across the pitch with a telephone message for me. There are people dead all over the place and they interrupt my leave to send me all the way here to look at this scene. What's special about this one, eh, Peterson?"

"Well, sir" Constable Peterson explained. "The doctor said it was a heart attack but it was the look of horror on the face yer see, sir. All twisted up like something ghastly. And it was the question of why she'd be out here at all overnight. Sounds like foul play to me sir, as sure as eggs is eggs. Anyway, I was told to guard what's left of the scene until yer got here."

"Hmmph" Inspector Bagthorpe snorted. "Heart problems and intense pain can easily cause the face to contort into a rictus grin. But I grant you, I can't think what anyone should be doing out here at night. I'll have a look".

He bent down, peering intently at the ground and every so often poking the leaves of the surrounding shrubs and trees, occasionally giving an 'hmm' and once or twice an 'aha!' followed by murmurs of disappointment.

"Have you found any footprints, sir?" Constable Peterson asked, peering over the Inspector's shoulder to see what he was looking at. "We might be able to match them to someone's shoes and catch the culprit."

"No, of course I haven't found any footprints" the Inspector grumbled. "The ground has been dry. There are patches where the grass has been trodden down more than others, but goodness only knows what you buffoons have done with the site. You should have left the body here for me to study, rather than lumbering all over the place and shipping it off as soon as you could. It makes it nearly impossible to establish anything further here".

He stood up, looking rather irked and brushed down the knees of his cricket trousers.

"How about this, sir?" Peterson cried. He ruffled around in a nearby bush. "It looks like a piece of cloth, sir.
I expect it belongs to the villain and was torn off in their haste to escape the scene of the crime."

"I shouldn't have thought so, Peterson" Inspector Bagthorpe said dryly. "Unless the assailant was wearing a pigeon upon his head. It looks remarkably

like a feather to me."
"Oh, of course sir. Ha! Silly mistake, my eyesight you see."

"Have the family and friends been questioned? Anyone come forward as to why she ventured out here in the middle of the night?"

"We d-did ask her relatives and neighbours, sir. But I'm afraid we couldn't get any sense out of 'em. They all said the same; that she'd have no reason to be here in the woods."

"Well, one of them is probably lying" the inspector sniffed, moustache bobbing up and down. "You can leave this scene now; it can't offer me anything else. I suppose that's the end of my match then, there's no chance of my getting back to it now. They put me down as 'retired out' anyway, which I *don't* find particularly flattering for a man of my deportment". He picked up his cricket bat and swung it disconsolately.
"If you'd be so good as to show me to your local station, I'll set myself up there right away and we can organise some more enquiries."
"Very good sir" Peterson replied, and the two men walked away.

The children waited with bated breath until they could no longer hear the receding footsteps before emerging from their hiding place.

"Why did they say this is the scene?" Lawrence was confused.

"This wasn't near the glade where we saw the ritual. It's much further on and deeper into the woods".
"I know" Rachel tucked her hair behind her ear and folded her arms. "So there's something going on."
"I'll say!" Lawrence said sardonically. "Someone's dropped dead in the woods and we're in the thick of it. This is just champion."
"Well, we're here now. We need to get to the bottom of it"
"Perhaps Margery's death was a coincidence?" Lawrence suggested hopefully. "Perhaps she really *did* die in this spot, and it was nothing to do with the… witchcraft. Apparently she was old – it could've just been a heart attack like the inspector said."

Rachel raised an eyebrow.
"It still doesn't tell us what she was doing out here at night. Suppose something happened at the ritual and they decided to cover it up and move the body so the police wouldn't find the evidence?"
"I can't imagine anything like that happening here, in such a quiet village" Lawrence remarked.
"Neither could I" agreed Rachel, "but then I couldn't have imagined anything like what we saw the other night either, but it happened. The only way to be sure is to find the place and take a look".

With trepidation, they continued their journey through the trees, while Rachel lamented in irritated whispers the impracticality of wearing a skirt.
"I've so many scratches on my legs now! I wish I had trousers like the Land Girls!"
Lawrence laughed despite his concern.

"I'm not sure Mrs Fernley would approve. Her idea of fashion seems to come from the Victorian era"
Rachel knew he was nervous; he didn't normally make such jokes, but he was obviously trying his best to seem brave even though he was terrified. Even she was worried. The thought of returning to the place where they had felt such inexplicable fear was horrifying, but there was no turning back. They had to, or else they would never know what had happened that night, and she believed that the key was in finding some sort of evidence in that glade.

A crow squawked and flew over their heads with a menacing rustle of feathers, making them jump. The atmosphere grew tense, and they walked tentatively, ready to turn and run at the slightest sign of danger. It was as if all the wildlife in the woods, and even the very trees, were holding their breath and waiting on tenterhooks for something to happen.

"Here we are" Rachel breathed as they emerged into the circular area where the ritual had taken place. They peeked from side to side to check they were alone before stepping fully into the open.
The glade's circular outline was strangely symmetrical, and was protected by the thick forest all around it.
It was eerily quiet, and they couldn't even hear the birds any more. It was almost like walking into a bubble. The tension in the air was palpable. They sniffed, and caught a waft of an unusual smell; a blend of the smoky scent that comes after you blow out a match, mixed with herbs and something with a slightly bitter tinge.

The charred remains of a fire were clearly visible in the centre of the glade, and scattered around the edge were grains of what looked like salt.

"See!" Rachel hissed triumphantly. "Here's the evidence! Now we have to tell the police and bring them here."

But before they could argue or decide how they would explain themselves, the decision to inform the authorities was taken out of their hands.

"Aha! What's going on here then? What are you kids up to?"

Constable Peterson had returned.

"I just directed an inspector from Scotland Yard back to the police station, then I came back into the woods to check – I *knew* I heard something," he continued. "What are you kids doing messing about in here?"

"S- Sorry, sir" Lawrence gibbered. "We didn't know it was out of bounds. We just came for a walk"

"Well, young man – what's yer name? You're one of the evacuee children aren't yer?"
"Yes, sir. My name's Lawrence and this is Rachel."
"Well then, Master Lawrence and Miss Rachel. The woods aren't out of bounds, but don't yer know there's been an unexplained death? We'd prefer not to have anyone wandering about in here, it could be dangerous"

“Yes sir, we heard” Rachel piped up. “In fact, that’s why we came, and we’ve got something to tell you.”

Lawrence’s heart sank.

“Oh yes?” Constable Peterson asked with condescension. “And what might that be?”

“We saw something strange the night they say Margery died, Constable” she began. “We looked out of the window of Mrs Fernley’s cottage, that’s the lady we’re staying with, because we couldn’t sleep and heard a noise. We saw a group of people walking into the woods all dressed in robes and carrying strange things.

So we followed them and they were holding hands in a circle with a fire in the middle. There was a woman chanting odd words and sweeping the ground with a broom, and then suddenly the fire went out, there was a scream and then there was… total darkness.
We ran home as fast as we could, and then we heard in the morning that Margery had been found dead”.

As she spoke, her words tumbled out faster and faster with increasing urgency until she was almost panting by the end of her explanation.

Constable Peterson looked as though he wasn’t sure whether to chuckle or to get cross.

“And what proof do you have of this, young lady?” he demanded.

"Look!" Rachel said, pointing at the remains of the fire and salt. "This proves we saw something here."
The policeman frowned sternly.
"That's the remains of a gypsy camp by the looks of it" he explained to them as if they were simpletons. "I know yer aren't used to the way things are in the country, but we get plenty of gypsies coming through these forests and setting up a fire for a while. That must be what yer saw. Look here," he strode over and dabbed a piece of ash with his finger, studying it closely.
"It's clear to me that they cooked sausages over this campfire approximately 36 hours ago".

Rachel and Lawrence looked at each other.
"Honestly, sir!" Rachel protested, dismayed at his attitude. "I'm not making it up, I swear. We felt a dark presence when the fire went out and it was terrifying. It's hard to explain. Look" she had a sudden flash of inspiration and pointed to her legs, "look at all these scratches.
I got these while we were running so fast in the dark to get away"

Constable Peterson frowned.
"Yer could have got those anywhere, climbing a tree or some such nonsense" he said gravely. "Maybe yer got scared by the gypsies and that's why yer ran. I think my superiors would take this very seriously if they knew yer were making up these fanciful tales. What do yer say to all this this, sonny?" he directed the last at Lawrence.
Lawrence had remained silent up to this point but reluctantly knew he had to back Rachel up.

"It's true, sir. I was there too and we know they weren't gypsies. They were dressed in robes and singing, like a – a spell."

"Well, gypsies probably do all that too" Constable Peterson was impatient. "And I don't want to hear another word about it. If yer don't want me to tell Mrs Fernley about yer mischief, then I suggest yer both stop this game right now or yer'll regret it"

The children could see there was no point in protesting further. They allowed themselves to be ushered out of the glade, promising dutifully that they wouldn't make up any more 'fantastic stories', as the policeman called it.

"See! I told you" Lawrence furiously nudged Rachel once the pompous Constable had left them on the lane at the outskirts of the woods.
"Look what trouble we could have got ourselves into! What are we going to do if Mrs Fernley finds out? What will my mother and father say?"

"It was worth a try" Rachel protested. "It's not my fault he's swallowed a Sherlock Holmes novel and thinks he's a detective. It was only right that we told him, because we know what we saw and justice should be done for Margery. They *always* ask witnesses to come forward."
"Not when it involves witchcraft" muttered Lawrence bitterly.

"Pssst!" came a sudden whisper from within the trees.
"What the dickens?" Lawrence jumped.

"Pssst!" it came again. "Over here!"

The children were startled by the sight of a white-haired old man gesturing wildly at them from behind an oak tree. They looked at each other nervously, wondering what new trouble this was.
"Don't be afraid" the man croaked. "Come closer!"

Lawrence and Rachel were unsure what to do.
"Come with me" the man urged, beckoning to them. "We have to go deeper into the forest"

Lawrence's knees shook but he was determined not to show it. He was grumpy about the trouble Rachel was getting them both into, and his annoyance overtook his nerves.
"Who the devil are you?" he asked bravely. "We're not going into the forest with you. We've only just come out of there after nearly being arrested"
"Yes, I saw all that" the man eyed him sharply. "That's what we have to talk about. I know you saw something the other night. You've been poking around"
"You've been watching us!" Rachel said, outraged.
"I can tell you what's going on, but for pity's sake hurry up before someone sees us!"

Wondering what awaited them, Rachel stepped forward first. Lawrence grabbed her sleeve and tried to pull her back.
"We don't know who this old fellow is!" he whispered urgently. "He could be a lunatic, and he certainly looks like one!"

“But he knows what happened” Rachel insisted. “He’s old, and there are two of us. You want to find out what’s going on, don’t you?”

Lawrence cursed his bad luck at being sent to this particular place at this particular time, with this particular girl. Why couldn’t he have been evacuated on his own to a friendly old couple at the seaside who treated him like another grandchild, bought him ice cream and took him to museums? Life would have been so much easier.
Taking a deep breath, he followed Rachel into the woods after the strange gesturing man.

“What do you want?” he asked, but the man held up a bony, bird-like hand.
“Phhst!” he hissed. “All in good time. Let’s get somewhere more private first”

“Yes, somewhere private so he can do us in, I expect” Lawrence whispered to Rachel, heart pounding. “Suppose he murdered Margery Blackthorn and now wants to do away with us?”

“Ahem” the old man coughed. “Despite my age, I have exceptionally good hearing you know.”

The children’s eyes met in mortification.

“Don’t worry” he croaked merrily, as if nothing had been said. “Now, we should be safe from prying eyes and ears”.
The children looked around in wonder as they realised where they were.

They were standing in a mystical little nook in the middle of the forest, surrounding by gnarled, ancient trees clothed in moss. Myriad birds twittered and they could hear the trickling of a nearby stream. A squirrel bustled into a hollow of an oak, and leaves draped with dewdrop pearls rustled with the foraging of hedgehogs. Insects hummed busily and frogs gave their throaty, reverberating call. It was a place entirely ruled by nature, forgotten by time.
"Well, come in then!" the mysterious man interrupted their observations. They looked around in bafflement. He had disappeared.
"Where's he gone?" Rachel asked, bewildered.

"Over here!" the voice came again, and they finally understood that they were standing in front of an entrance to a tiny cave entirely hidden by the overhanging boughs of a weeping willow.
A gentle parting of the leaves revealed the white-haired man perched like a gnome inside a strange grotto on a bench hewn out of the rock.
They entered nervously, goggling at the stone shelves filled with colourful bottles and trinkets, and a small fire over which a large, black kettle hung and bubbled away industriously. It was like the lair of a witch or a hobgoblin.

"Be not afeard," the eccentric character recited, "for the woods are full of noises. Sounds and sweet airs that give delight and hurt not. Sometimes a thousand twangling instruments will hum about mine ears and sometime voices that, if I had then waked after long sleep, will make me sleep again."

"*The Tempest*" Lawrence announced. "But I think it should actually go 'be not afeard for the *isle* is full of noises".

"But what does it mean*?"* interrupted Rachel. Her impatient nature made her wish people would just speak plainly rather than spouting half-baked riddles.

"No matter" the elderly man waved his hand dismissively. "The point still stands. I'm not a madman quoting Shakespeare for the sake of it. You really shouldn't be 'afeard', because these woods *are* full of noises, music and magic.
What you think you see and understand may not be what it seems. The old ways reign supreme here, and when respected, bring only peace."

"You're not making any sense" Rachel complained, taking in his odd appearance with curious eyes. He was shabbily dressed in a grubby overcoat and was hunched over, clinging to a stick despite being seated. He wore a pair of half-moon spectacles over which he peered with dark, beady eyes that were almost black and seemingly bottomless – eyes you could get lost in if you weren't careful. Both children now felt he was probably harmless enough, but were still on their guard as they perceived that he had an edge to him that meant they couldn't fully trust him yet.

"My name's Gerald Gardner" he stated simply. "I'm a member of the coven here at Burley. I used to live in Christchurch but came here so I could join other like-minded souls and play my part."

When the children didn't react, he looked at them keenly to check that they understood.
"I'm a witch".
"A witch?" Lawrence was confused. "I thought witches were women. If you really were any such thing, wouldn't you be a wizard or warlock?"
Gerald gave a scratchy laugh.
"No. A lot of people think that, but the correct term is 'witch', whether male or female. The word 'wizard' makes one sound like Merlin. Ridiculous."

A few weeks ago, had Lawrence and Rachel been ushered into a cave and regaled with stories of witches, they would have thought him a perfect madman. But now, after their strange experience in the woods, they were not unduly surprised, and were willing to accept that mysterious things were happening in Burley.

"Well, what do you want to talk to us for?" Rachel pressed him. "Were you part of that magic ritual? And what happened to Margery Blackthorn? Did you kill her?" her eyes flashed with sudden anger.

Gerald stood up remarkably straight despite his reliance on his stick, and anger swept his face.
"We've never killed anybody! Accuse us of anything but that. Throughout the ages, people like us have been persecuted and murdered. True followers of the craft would never rise to violence, despite the abominable treatment we have received."
He visibly reined himself in and sat down on the stone bench once more.
"If you sit there quietly, I'll explain everything."

There was nothing to be done but sit cross-legged on the dusty floor inside that mysterious grotto, swathed in its forest cocoon, and listen to Gerald's story.

Chapter 6

1990

Molly and Nick had been engrossed in Rachel Morgan's diary for so long that they had lost track of time, and were surprised when a key turned in the lock downstairs and a voice called out,
"I'm home! Are you in, Molly?"

Molly jumped to her feet. "That time already!"

She clattered her way down the spiral stairs still clutching the diary, closely followed by Nick.
"Hey Mum" she crossed her fingers that her mother wouldn't say or do anything to embarrass her. She was brilliant, but no less eccentric than Miss Clutterbuck next door, in her own way.
"Who's this then?" Mrs Morgan enquired.
"I'm Nick – I'm staying with my Aunt Clarissa next door for a while. My parents are moving us down here permanently. Molly invited me over, I hope that's alright".

"Pleased to meet you, Nick, and welcome to Burley. I'm sure you've fallen in love with the place already?" she held out her hand for him to shake, and he couldn't help but stare at her long nails, painted purple and adorned with tiny white crescent moons. He counted at least three rings on her fingers, one of which was in the shape of a five-pointed star. Clusters of shiny bangles clinked on her wrists, and when he looked up to take in her appearance fully,

he thought she must have walked straight out of the 1970's with her tie-dyed tasselled bag and long, flowery skirt which trailed the floor.
"Er – yes" he stuttered, nonplussed. "It's…um…a really nice village". He had never seen anyone quite like her before, not just in her manner of dress but her demeanour. He couldn't have put it into words, but she seemed floaty and ethereal somehow, and there was something in her presence that was effortlessly calming.

"Well, it's good for Molly to have a friend around. I hope she's been making you feel welcome. What were you doing up there, anyhow?"

"We found gran's old diary!" Molly interrupted, brimming with eagerness to talk about what they had discovered. "She wrote about how she was evacuated here in the war with a boy called Lawrence, and they witnessed a witchcraft ritual in the woods here one night and then a woman was found dead there the next day. They tried to tell the police but they didn't believe them, and then we've just got to the bit where they've met the *actual Gerald Gardner!"*
"You know who Gerald Gardner is?" Nick asked, baffled.
"Yes, I was just about to tell you when Mum came home"
"You found her diary?" Mrs Morgan was astonished. "I didn't even know she had one. She never told me much about her life here as an evacuee. Where was it?"
"We weren't poking around or anything, promise" Molly responded.

"One of those dusty old boxes got knocked over and we found it in there"

"Hmm, I'm surprised I never stumbled across it before" Mrs Morgan drifted towards the kitchen. "Let's not stand around talking in the hallway. Anyone want herbal tea? Nick?"

"Um… yes, thank you. But who's this Gerald Gardner character?"

"He was a Wiccan, or what you would call a witch" Molly answered. "He lived all around the world and had a colourful history, but what gran wrote in the diary was true – at one point he lived in Christchurch and was apparently initiated into the New Forest coven at the Mill House in Highcliffe, and spent a lot of time here in Burley."
"I'm not even going to ask what a coven is, or how he was initiated."
"Good. Anyway, people say that he took part in something that helped the war effort, although I'm not sure what, and he was also in the Home Guard. He's very well-known in the area, and he owned a witchcraft museum. I think he died sometime in the 60's."

"That's right." Mrs Morgan reappeared bearing a tray of three mugs. "Why don't you both come through into the living room and sit down?
Anyway I'm surprised you don't know all this, Nick – do you know the name of the woman who initiated him into the New Forest coven?"

Molly tensed and she tried to shake her head subtly at her mother to stop her blurting it out; she had deliberately omitted that part of the explanation.

"Dorothy Clutterbuck" Mrs Morgan forged ahead anyway with a breezy smile.

Nick looked confused.
"Clutterbuck? As in, this person was probably related to my Aunt Clarissa Clutterbuck? Who lives next door?"

"Yes, of course! Didn't you know? There aren't too many Clutterbucks around"

"Are you telling me my aunt is a witch?" he laughed. "That's ridiculous. I know she's strange, but…"
He trailed off. "You mean it, don't you?"

Mrs Morgan nodded. "I didn't intend to shock you" she said. "I assumed you knew all about it"

Nick shook his head. "What on *earth* is going on here? Um, hello? The 1600's called, they want their witches back."

Molly tried not to laugh, half-worried and half-amused by Nick's reaction.

Mrs Morgan took a sip of her tea while Nick sat in silence. After a moment, he asked, "This isn't a joke, is it?"
Molly's mum shook her head and looked serious.
Nick put his head in his hands and groaned.

"How did I get myself into this?" he mumbled.

Molly clutched her mug of tea tightly, not sure what to say or do.

Nick looked up, apparently having made the decision to believe them. "Does that mean my mum is a witch too?"

"No, of course not!" Mrs Morgan gave a delicate, tinkling laugh. "It's not hereditary you know! Having someone in your family who practices witchcraft doesn't make you a witch too. It's a choice you make, whether you wish to follow the path or not. Likewise, there's nothing to stop someone who has never even met a witch from becoming one. We don't run around in black hats and cast spells with a magic wand, if that's what you think. It's nothing of the sort."

Nick stopped short. "What do you mean, "we"? Are you…a witch too?"

"Yes of course I am, dear. Didn't you know?"

1990
Molly

My heart sank down to somewhere around my feet when mum opened her mouth and started telling Nick that not only is she a witch, but his aunt is related to one of the founding members of the New Forest coven. I couldn't believe it – she normally keeps it to herself; like I said before, a lot of people still don't understand. But here she was, gabbling away without a second thought. When I challenged her later, she said that any friend of mine was a friend of hers. "Yes" I had gritted my teeth in frustration, "But I've only known him for two days! I don't normally care what others think, but enough people around here think we're weird, so it would have been nice to at least *seem* normal for a while."

As it happened, Nick had taken the news remarkably well. For someone who had been dragged to this village in the middle of the forest from his lifelong home in London, and who clearly had very little interest in the esoteric or even in nature, he had been really quite calm. Or maybe he was just in shock.

"Why didn't you tell me?" he had asked after the initial disbelief had worn off, gingerly sipping his tea. His face contorted and he looked at it in distaste.

"It's camomile, dear" mum told him calmly, as though nothing had happened.

“I thought you wouldn’t understand” I replied, looking down at the floor. “Most don’t, and they think that people like mum are evil. It’s not like that at all. And you seem to hate Burley so much and you’re used to such a different life in London, I thought you wouldn’t want anything to do with me if you knew”

“Well, I know you’re not evil” he said, sounding a bit sheepish. “I’m just a bit… surprised. I honestly didn’t think witchcraft was real. I know they used to burn and hang people but I never believed there was anything in it”.

“A lot of people don’t” mum reassured him. “And sadly, most of those who were murdered throughout the ages – men too, not just women – had never done anything to harm anyone. That’s not what it’s about, you see.”
“So what is it exactly, if it’s not curses and flying on broomsticks?”

“Lots of them probably used herbal remedies for healing and were viewed with suspicion and superstition bred from ignorance, and some of them didn’t have anything to do with witchcraft at all. But in those days, if your enemy in the village accused you of giving his cow a funny look, that was enough to get you arrested. People claimed these so-called witches could curdle milk just by walking past, or kill livestock with a stare.”

She paused to take a sip of her tea.

"A real historical example is the Salem witch trials in America towards the end of the 17th century, when innocent people were accused of witchcraft by their neighbours in order to steal their land. After they were hanged, the real truth was discovered but by that point, it was too late of course. An absolute travesty."

"I didn't know any of that" Nick said, opening his eyes wide. "So what exactly do you *do*, then?"

Gratified to have an opportunity to talk about her craft, mum beamed and launched into an enthusiastic monologue.

"There are all kinds of things, and we all have personal preferences. Mine is herbalism. It's not even really witchcraft; it's just being part of the circle of nature and respecting the earth. I studied botany when I was younger and I've always loved walking through the forest collecting ingredients. I make salves for cuts, bruises and burns as well as teas that help calm you down, improve digestion, enhance your concentration…."
Nick glanced anxiously at his mug.
"No, don't worry" she said with a smile. "That's a Twinings teabag, I didn't concoct that one!"

I continued where mum left off. "Some people like to use crystals instead. They can be cleansed and charged in different ways, and different stones are helpful for certain health problems or to improve an aspect of your life. Like obsidian, which is supposed to protect you from negative energy."

"So do witches actually hold ceremonies like the one in your gran's diary?"

"Some do. They usually start with casting a circle and saluting the four watchtowers. That means invoking the power of the elements, so Air in the East, Fire in the South, Water in the West and Earth in the North. Sometimes they also call out to the energies of the above, the below and the sacred centre."

"But what's all that *for?"* Nick was none the wiser.

"It creates a sacred space" mum elaborated. "A circle is created for protection and to channel the energy of the elements. Often, a physical circle will be marked out in salt or sometimes chalk. Once the spell or ritual is complete, they'll thank all the attendant elements or energies and then symbolically release them. The participants finish with a statement like, 'the circle is open, yet unbroken. Blessed be!'"

"I see" said Nick, although he didn't really. "Well that explains the circle and the salt. The diary also mentioned someone sweeping the ground with a broom. What would that have been about?"

"It was probably to sweep away any negative energy" I interjected. "And they're usually called 'besoms' rather than brooms. But the point is, these sorts of things are about channelling positive energy and respecting all life. So why was somebody found dead the next day?"

Chapter 7

1940

Lawrence and Rachel sat transfixed inside Gerald's mystical grotto, apprehensive yet intrigued. The overhanging willow branches blocked out most of the light, but a few sunbeams filtered through, illuminating the dancing dust motes in the air. Birds twittered in the distance, the sound muffled inside the cave.

The mysterious man cleared his throat.

"What you are about to hear may surprise you" he warned them, leaning forward conspiratorially. "And you must never, ever speak of it to anyone. I need you to promise that right now. The very safety of our country may depend upon it"

The children gave their solemn vows, knowing that this was the only way they could find out what was going on.

"We also need your help" the old man continued.

"With what, exactly?" Rachel demanded. "What if we refuse?"

Gerald eyed them regretfully. "I'm afraid it's rather dangerous. The death of poor Margery Blackthorn vouches for that. But there's no choice.

And I think we would all be sorry if you refused to help, because I would have no option but to tell your guardian – Mrs Fernley, isn't it? – about your antics in the woods. Suppose somebody also told Constable Peterson that you had been spotted in the forest that fateful night, and gave it on good authority that you had been creeping around with intent to cause mischief, jumped out on poor Margery and scared her so much that she suffered a heart attack?" he shook his head. "We wouldn't want that, would we?"

"You – you crook!" Lawrence spluttered. "You know that's not true! That's blackmail!"

"I wouldn't call it that, exactly" Gerald tugged at his bushy, white beard. "It's no more blackmail than it is for the government to conscript men into the army, sending them to their deaths whether they like it or not. We all know that if they object, they are taken to a tribunal and are often publicly ridiculed or worse. What's that, if it's not blackmail? If you listen, you'll understand. This is for the sake of the war effort and the security of our futures".

"Alright, then" Rachel turned up her nose proudly. "What do you want from us?"

Gerald shuffled on the stone bench before continuing in his scratchy voice.

"It's called Operation Cone of Power. It must forever be kept secret. If it ever does come out, most people won't believe it anyway.

We've had a strong coven of witches here in the New Forest for many years, and we have a plan to make our own contribution to the war effort.

Everyone knows the worst of all fears is for Germany to launch an invasion onto British soil. They've already started invading the Ardennes and the Low Countries in the last couple of months, so how long will it be before they try to cross the Channel? And then where will we be – speaking in German and saluting those jackbooted monsters?"

Lawrence swallowed. "Well, what is this Operation – whatever it was. What's it *for*?"

"We intend to join as many as we can in a circle, and direct our energy towards Germany, sending a message to their High Command that they won't even realise they've received. With the cone of power we generate together, we will send waves towards them that infiltrate their minds and make them realise that an attempt to cross the Channel would be a failure, that an invasion of England would be fruitless and lead to unacceptable loss of German life. We'll send this message to them so strongly that those in power will make the decision not to attempt it. And in so doing, we beat them – and they won't know a thing about it".

"But how would that work?" asked Rachel, lip curled in scepticism.

"You tell me" Gerald smirked in a way that made him look rather like a predatory animal.

"Over the last few minutes I've been sending positive energy towards you two to make you feel more trusting towards me, and invigorated to join us in the fight"

Their shocked silence spoke volumes as they both realised his words had just described exactly how they felt, although some disbelief and confusion remained.

"How on earth did you do that?" Lawrence whistled. "I mean, obviously it's worked but I don't understand *how"*

"You don't need to worry about how. Only that it can be done on the far larger scale that we intend, but on the condition that we have enough people working together. I'm afraid that without Margery, we will be slightly short. I believe you must join us to ensure our success"

"But why do you need us?" Rachel asked, confused. "Why can't you ask another adult from the village?"

"There is no-one left in the village to whom we can appeal; all who are sympathetic to our cause have already joined us, and it would be dangerous to place our trust in any who remain unaware. Children have a special kind of essence, an as yet unbroken spirit and innocence that can be very powerful if channelled correctly. Somehow I feel that the only way is for you two to help us."
Rachel and Lawrence knew each other's anxious expression was a mirror of their own.

"I want to help" Rachel admitted, somewhat penitently. "And we'll do what we can. But how did Margery die? Are people often hurt when attempting this sort of thing?"

"Now that is our gravest concern" Gerald frowned, his forehead wrinkling like a piece of old parchment. "That ritual the other night was a meeting to generate and cultivate our energy, to draw on the force of the earth in preparation. Call it a rehearsal for the real thing, if you like. As you no doubt remember, seeing as you were there hiding in the bushes at the time like thieves in the night, there was a sudden uproar when the fire went out, and a petrifying, overwhelming feeling of blackness. Devilish, demonic. Whatever you like to call it. We believe there is an evil witch at work – certainly not one of our number."

"But how do you know that someone from your group isn't the evil witch?" Lawrence asked.

"As I've said before, the only tenet of our work is to harm none. Anyone who does otherwise is not deserving of the name, and would never have been allowed to join our coven. However, as with everything in life, there is always a balance and some will invariably turn towards the dark.

With the force of that negative power, the ritual was interrupted and the circle was broken, just for a moment. Margery must have dropped the hands of the others on each side of her, making her vulnerable to attack. Oh yes, it will appear like heart failure of some kind to any doctor who examines her, but we all know there was a wave of dark magic that night."

"Why was her body found elsewhere?" Lawrence asked nervously, remembering what they had seen less than an hour earlier. "Did you move it?"

"I'm afraid we had to" Gerald grimaced. "As it turned out, the good Constable Peterson would never have put two and two together anyway, even if he had found her body in the middle of the salt-strewn clearing amid the remains of a fire whilst a bearded loon in a cloak murmured incantations over her. But the Scotland Yard chap might have wondered. To be honest, I'm surprised he didn't look further.
We only had the opportunity to move poor Margery and didn't have time to clear away the circle without attracting suspicion but fortunately it's so deep into the woods that it's unlikely anyone would stumble across it. Anyway, as you saw for yourselves earlier, people believe what they want to anyway. Gypsies! I ask you. Anyway, it's imperative that our work remains secret, just like *all* work for the war effort, which is why we couldn't take any chances with her body."

Lawrence set his jaw firmly. He felt funny being the one to ask all the questions, but he was determined to understand what was going on.

"If your work is so secret" he asked, "then how does the evil witch know about it? Could there be a spy in your ranks? I've read about these sorts of things in books."

"And why would anyone, evil witch or not, want to stop you trying to win the war anyway?" Rachel joined in.

"We're not entirely sure" the old man pondered, stroking his stick with skeletal fingers. "But we have a strong theory. There was a man - a witch - who lived here in Burley. In 1916, the middle of the First World War, the government had just brought in its policy of conscription, and there was a terrible incident. This man, named Thomas Wetherby, was a conscientious objector and vocally so. One night, he entered into a disagreement with some men at the public house who were celebrating their last night on British soil before being dispatched to join the fight, and they found his pacifism objectionable. One thing led to another, and I'm afraid Thomas was killed in the ensuing fracas."

"That's an irony" Rachel muttered, thoughts lingering on her own father's conscientious objection to war, and those who ridiculed him. "A pacifist killed in a fight!"

"Yes. Odd, isn't it, how things go? Anyway, whether they knew he was a witch or not, and whether that had any bearing on their reaction to him, who can tell? But the fact was, he was always something of a loose cannon, so to speak, despite his pacifism. I met him once when I was younger, and he was very opinionated, very tricky to deal with. His objection to the war was more to do with his contrariness than conscience, and he was a very angry young man, unable to accept the loss of his father who was killed fighting in the Boer War in 1901. We believe that Thomas Wetherby's dark spirit somehow lingers here, his unresolved anger directed at England and everything it stands for. The way he sees it, and one can almost understand why, is that wars have done him no favours. Fighting had in very different ways got both him and his father killed – and for what? He probably doesn't understand why our coven is participating in the war and wants to sabotage our attempt, not caring who he harms in doing so. To him, a German invasion would seem almost poetic justice for everything that happened to him".

Lawrence eventually spoke.
"That's all very well" he began. "But how does all this 'dark spirit' business work? I mean, how do you expect us to believe all that?"

Gerald eyed him carefully. "Well, you believe what happened in the forest that night, don't you? You experienced that for yourself."

"Alright" Lawrence agreed, turning it over in his mind. "But how do you know what Thomas Wetherby is thinking, and what his motives are? You seem to have dreamed up quite a story. I mean, he's dead for goodness sake, so how can he be 'thinking' anything?"

After the words had left his mouth, Lawrence felt surprised at his own daring. Usually more content to stay on the sidelines and keep his nose in a book, reading tales of derring-do, not actually *participating* in them, he realised that whether he liked it or not, he was inextricably involved in this now, and he might as well do his best to get to the bottom of it.

"Some of us remember the news of his being killed" Gerald replied. "So that's a fact. As to his still lingering and directing anger towards us, one of our members attempted to scry for the answer – that's the practice of seeking images using a mirror or crystal for instance. She saw snatches of what I've explained, and felt his power which remains around the earth even though his physical body is long gone. She spent two days in bed, struck down with a terrible migraine and nausea triggered by the intense feelings of evil she experienced while trying to reach his spirit. And that's not all. We discovered that the men who were involved in Thomas's murder all died in mysterious circumstances within a year of the incident. Was it all a strange coincidence? Perhaps. But we think not."

"What exactly were these mysterious circumstances?" asked Lawrence hesitantly, not entirely sure that he wanted to know the answer.

"I shan't go into all the grisly details" Gerald said, his concern evident as he absently fiddled with his stick. "But suffice it to say there were a number of, shall we say, *unusual* accidents. The men were all fighting in the war, so one might have expected them to be killed, but it wasn't the usual dangers that finished them off. For instance, one of them was run over by a reversing tractor in a field, while another fell to his death when his parachute disintegrated in mid-air."

An involuntary shiver swept through Lawrence and Rachel. They were dumbfounded at how their evacuation into the quiet countryside could have resulted in their enlistment into a coven of witches who were trying to fight off a German invasion, as well as having a murderous spirit bearing down on them.

“So, will you join us?” Gerald prompted them, peering at them intently with his beady eyes.

“I don’t know about that” Lawrence began, but Rachel met Gerald’s gaze resolutely.
“We’ll do it” she said.
“Nancy Drew to the rescue.” Lawrence muttered.

On the way back to Mrs Fernley’s cottage, they talked about the events of the day and struggled to understand how they could have been swept up so suddenly into this bizarre series of events. Before the war, neither would have believed that any of this was even possible and would have laughed at anyone who suggested it.

“I expect one day an awful lot of stories will be written about children’s adventures when they were evacuated during the war” Lawrence said. “We seem to have ended up with the most dangerous one. I wonder what other dramas are playing out up and down the country? There are probably some lucky kids out there who have found a magic portal into another world through a wardrobe or something like that, and we’re here risking our lives with a bunch of witches to thwart a German invasion. Typical!”

Later that evening, after a rather tasteless meal of spam, potatoes and cauliflower, Rachel and Lawrence listened distractedly to the BBC radio broadcast with Mrs Fernley. The news was grim; all women and children had been ordered to evacuate Gibraltar and the USSR had annexed Lithuania. Although these places sounded distant, the children knew that Britain was also at risk as Hitler's forces grew stronger, and their stomachs flipped whenever they remembered what they had to do to fight it. Partway through the broadcast, the radio suddenly switched itself off and the lamp flickered. Mrs Fernley looked up from her embroidery with a frown. She turned the radio on and off but it appeared to be completely dead. She shivered, pulling her cardigan closer around herself.
"It's come over rather cold, all of a sudden" she said, surprised.
Rachel agreed, folding her arms to keep in the fading warmth. Lawrence glanced around nervously, on edge after their conversation with Gerald Gardner about the dark witch who desired to thwart their plans.

The chill in the air was more intense than that generated by a merely draughty house – and besides, it was the middle of summer. It had come on suddenly, and within moments they began to feel it penetrating through to their very bones. Lawrence felt it in his chest like a cold hand reaching in and clenching his heart.
The lights flickered again and Rachel jumped.

"That's peculiar" Mrs Fernley said, reaching for her shawl and putting it on over her cardigan.

"Perhaps it's best we all retire to bed and keep warm, the weather's obviously taken a turn for the worse".

No sooner had she spoken than the air in the room seemed to shimmer and a strange scent reached their nostrils. Rachel sniffed. She wasn't sure what it was, but she had an inkling that it was something like gunpowder and tobacco. Lawrence was thinking the same, as it smelt a little like the pungent, sulphurous air on Guy Fawkes night after fireworks had been let off.

As they gazed transfixed, the image of a man slowly appeared before them. A man dressed in old-fashioned clothes, as if from the 17th or 18th century; ruffled shirt and breeches with muskets at his side and a feather in his hat. He stood, or rather *wavered* before them, not quite there but not quite as ghostly as horror stories might describe. Other than the slight shifting of air and the pervasive chill he brought with him, he seemed almost as real as anyone.

Nobody moved. All three simply stared, gaping at the being before them. The apparition opened its mouth, and the single word he spoke sent cold chills scuttling up and down their spines.

"Beware".

Mrs Fernley stifled a scream, and Rachel and Lawrence clasped each other's hand for dear life.
It was as if the mysterious figure had used all his energy to deliver this warning, as once he had spoken, he shimmered once more and appeared less

substantial. The lights flickered off, and in the split second of darkness before they sparked back into life, he had disappeared.

The icy fingers of fear receded from their hearts as the air gradually began to warm. They looked at each other, but did not speak. Not one of them knew what to say. But underneath the immediate shock, confusion and the whys and wherefores, the children knew deep down which danger they were being warned about. Rachel was so unsettled by the events of the evening that she didn't even write about it in her diary. Putting events and thoughts into words had the extraordinary and sometimes unwelcome effect of making them feel more real.

Right now, even thoughts of German bombers and air-raid shelters seemed more appealing than the notion of ghostly warnings – at least they were full of the sounds, sights and gritty emotions of life, and everyone in the country was feeling the same.
With Gerald Gardner's looming witchcraft ritual which they were forbidden to discuss with a single soul, and now the apparition of an ominous spectre, Rachel and Lawrence were beginning to feel horribly, achingly alone in this war.

Chapter 8

1990

Still reeling from his sudden immersion into the world of witchcraft, Nick was unsettled at the thought of a woman being found dead in Burley the morning after the terrifying events Rachel Morgan had described in her diary. He understood that witchcraft wasn't meant to be evil in any way, and was in fact quite the opposite. But *something* must have happened that night. Despite only having been in Burley for a few days and still feeling homesick for London, he was intensely curious to discover the truth. After all, he had always enjoyed people-watching from the balcony, imagining what life was like for the woman with three poodles, where the man with the umbrella was going, and why the teenager with blue hair looked so angry. Any human story was interesting, and this one seemed more unusual than most.

Finishing the floral and surprisingly calming camomile tea, he stood up.
"Thank you for the drink, Mrs Morgan" he rose and made for the door, "but I should get back next door or my aunt will wonder where I am."
"That's all right, and it was nice to meet you Nick. But please, call me Lilianna. And you're welcome to come over tomorrow night to have dinner with me and Molly, if your aunt doesn't mind"
"That would be lovely Mrs Mor – er, Lilianna. Thank you". And to his surprise, he actually meant it.

That evening he decided to tell Aunt Clarissa about what he had learnt.
"I discovered something interesting today" he mumbled through a mouthful of bean soup which tasted strangely like bananas.
"Oh yes?" she lifted her lorgnette to her nose and peered at him. "What was that, then?"
"You know I said I'd met Molly next door – well, we were in her attic and we found her gran's old diary from when she was twelve and was an evacuee here during the war."
He decided not to broach the subject of witchcraft for now.
"Oh? Rachel Morgan, yes I knew her. She was quite a few years older than me. It was terribly sad when she died. She was only in her fifties, not very old at all really, but you know how cruel cancer can be."
"What was she like?"
"Molly is the spitting image of her. Long dark hair, green eyes, always talking. Loquacious, you might call it, but she became quieter, more reserved towards the end of her illness, poor thing. Although certain things she wouldn't talk about anyway, and never did."

Nick jumped and swore as a cat scratched his leg underneath the table.
"Naughty, naughty" Aunt Clarissa said, peering under the tablecloth.
"Yes, she is" Nick rubbed his leg. "That's the fourth time she's scratched me"
"No, I meant you. No swearing at the dinner table please" she wagged a plump finger.

Nick rolled his eyes.
"Alright, I'll stand in the middle of the kitchen and do it instead then"
"Don't be clever" his aunt warned him.
"Sorry. Anyway, I wondered if you knew about something she was involved with, something that happened here during the war. We read in the diary that Rachel and her friend Lawrence witnessed some kind of ritual in the forest and then the next day, a woman was found dead. Do you know what happened?"

Clarissa Clutterbuck's brow furrowed and she shook her head violently, making her bright purple earrings clink.

"No" she said vehemently. "I wouldn't know anything about it, seeing as I would have been less than four years old at the time".
"But you must have heard stories growing up?" Nick persisted.
"No" was the staunch reply. "I knew Rachel but I don't know anything about any witchcraft ritual or any dead people. Now look, you've upset Mr McTavish"

She picked up a grey, rather moth-eaten old cat that was prowling around looking for scraps, and stroked his fur reassuringly.
"Don't worry Mr McTavish" she crooned. "We won't talk any more about it".
And that, Nick realised, was that. For whatever reason, his aunt was unwilling to talk about the events of 1940, even though she would doubtless have heard

about it in her childhood. He thought it would be unwise to mention the Dorothy Clutterbuck of the coven and whether she was related. He didn't want to find himself forced into apologetically making Mr McTavish feel better with a flea comb and a rubber mouse.

1990
Molly

After Nick went home and mum and I had finished our dinner, I retreated back up to the attic to continue reading the diary. I hesitated for a moment, knowing that Nick would want to read it with me, but after wrestling with my conscience for a moment I went ahead anyway – it had belonged to *my* gran after all.

I lit an incense stick and breathed in the spicy aroma as I flipped to the page where we'd left off – the point where she and Lawrence had just sat down inside Gerald Gardner's forest grotto. The description of it made my mind race, envisioning what such a magical little cave would look like, hearing the gentle trickling of the nearby stream and the chirping of the forest birds, the scent of fresh, green leaves and rich, fruity earth. I wondered if the place was still there now, fifty years later, or whether it had been completely taken over by nature, populated only by the ghost of a breeze and the sense that something important had once happened there. I brought my attention back to the diary, butterflies dancing in my stomach in excitement as I wondered what I would discover. I turned the page and stopped, startled. Flicked through the next few pages to check I wasn't mistaken. Shook the diary upside down, in case any other folded papers were tucked inside. I couldn't believe it – the passage ended abruptly. I frantically skimmed the last part of the entry.

When this strange, white-bearded old man Mr Gardner began to explain everything to us, we were frightened. Frightened and confused. He spoke about the war effort and how they are planning something which could change the course of history. He warned us that dark forces are at work, and poor Margery Blackthorn had been killed by a rogue witch – but not one of their number. He told us they need our help, but before we could even think for ourselves whether we wanted to or not, he blackmailed us with the threat of telling Mrs Fernley what we'd been up to.

What choice do we have? Be sent home in disgrace back to the bombs and our parents' disapproval? Lawrence is especially worried about that. Anyway, there's nothing to be done. We've agreed to take part, and it will happen within the next week. He'll get a message to us somehow, he said. We've been sworn to secrecy so I won't write anything more about the details, just in case anyone was to ever find it. I don't see how I can write in this diary again anyway. How can I go drivelling on about everyday events like what we had for breakfast, while all the time having a secret – knowing that we're going to do something which will probably be the most momentous event of our lives?

I shook my head as waves of disappointment washed over me. The rest of the diary was simply full of blank pages. My gran had certainly kept her promise not to tell anyone, and she had been correct in her prediction about not wanting to write in her diary again.

I wondered why she had kept it at all instead of destroying it. A whimsical part of me thought perhaps she had half-hoped mum or I would find it one day and piece together enough clues to deduce what had happened, when the time was right. It seemed such a shame for the story to have gone to the grave with her, and for us to have learnt so much and suddenly be thwarted was disheartening. Laying the diary aside, I decided to distract myself by looking through the photos I'd taken earlier – on the way home with Nick I'd dropped them off at the shop to be developed, and mum had picked them up for me after work.

I didn't have much enthusiasm for it after the let-down of the diary, and scanned through them with little interest. The photos were nice enough to look at but nothing special. I was about to place them aside again when something caught my eye. One of the photos showed a man standing against a tree dressed in old-fashioned clothes – a white ruffled shirt, breeches and a neckerchief. I cracked a smile; this had happened once before when they'd got the photos mixed up and somebody else's holiday snaps had made their way into my pile.

It wasn't a very good picture anyway so I was sure whoever had taken it wouldn't miss it, it was grainy and made the man look like he wasn't quite there. I imagined it was probably a local costumed event or re-enactment of something, and I thought no more of it.

The following day, mum took me shopping in Ringwood and Nick spent the afternoon with his aunt, so I had to wait until the evening before I could break the news to him about the diary, which disappointed him almost as much as it had me. I suspected he was being drawn into the mystery like I was, and becoming less sulky about being in Burley, and although I had been worried about his reaction after finding out about the witchcraft the day before, he behaved as though nothing had happened, and I was grateful for his acceptance because I knew it would have been a lot for him to absorb. At the dinner table with mum and me, he told us more about himself and his family.

"Do you have any brothers or sisters, Nick?" mum asked.
"Yes, I have a brother" Nick replied, twirling spaghetti around his fork in what I conceded to be an expert manner. "He's older than me, at university in Birmingham studying anthropology. So he escaped our fate and didn't have to move here with us" he grinned, and we knew he was only joking now about the last part.
"He's very clever – always been better at things than me" he smiled sheepishly. "He was the one who was good at sports too. I've just always been clumsy."
"*That's* definitely true" I said.
"Molly! Don't be rude" mum chided me. "Go on, Nick"
"When we were little I was always the one who gave my parents a fit when they looked away for a second in the Tube station and I'd wandered off, just looking at things and watching the crowds.

I grew up in such a busy, noisy place that it's a massive shock for me to come and live somewhere so different. When I got older I started running errands for them but got distracted by all the things to watch and look at. Once I got into trouble for tagging along with a busker. I lost track of time and my dad came looking for me, only to find me sitting on the pavement learning chords on the guitar."

I chuckled to myself, finding it easy to believe as I remembered how he had persuaded me to let him 'tag along' when I went to take photos at the Old Mill. I remained uncharacteristically quiet while we ate, happy to let someone else chatter for a change and pleased that mum and Nick were getting on so well – I was sure my friend Eliza would welcome him too when she came back from her holiday. I had started out thinking that he was arrogant and a bit spoilt but in just a few short days that grumpy exterior had fallen away. But I still wished he would wear a clean sweater and cut his hair so it didn't keep falling all over his face.

I stopped my musings and came back to reality at the table. "What do your parents do?" my mum was asking.

"My mum and dad are both accountants, something to do with tax I think." Nick shrugged. "I don't know much about it to be honest. Maybe I should talk to them more" he said thoughtfully. "What do you do, Mrs Morgan, if you don't mind my asking?"

Mum's tinkling laugh rang out like a bell.

"Not at all. I work in a library. I source books for them, especially for the 'Mind, Body and Spirit' section – luckily they're quite relaxed which is how I get away with dressing like this. No boring black suits for me!" She pointed down at her outfit; another of her trailing patchwork skirts teamed with a loose purple top and a chunky silver amulet hanging from her neck depicting planets moving around the Sun.

"I read an article about libraries the other day, in a computer magazine" said Nick. "It was about how these experts are creating a galactic network of computers which will allow everyday people to access a whole web of information anywhere in the world. They say that we'll be able to send letters to each other in the blink of an eye or even read digital books instead of printed ones".

"That sounds very futuristic. Well, it's got to be a good thing as long as these computers don't completely replace real libraries. I'd be worried about my job if all this new technology takes off one day. We all like old-fashioned things in this house, take Molly's father for instance" Mrs Morgan said, taking a sip of her elderflower cordial.
"He's an antiques dealer. He's in Egypt at the moment, sniffing around the bazaars like a tenacious bloodhound. He's seen some strange places, I can tell you – odd things happen all around the world you know, sometimes even more mysterious than here in Burley."

I thought to myself that some of dad's exotic marketplaces would be an ideal location for a story –

I still want to be a photographer but now I've started writing all this down,
I've decided that being an author might be quite fun after all. But to describe these places *properly* I'd have to go there myself. Maybe one day I'll persuade him to take me along. If Burley can be home to a vast array of myth, magic and mystery, just imagine what could be waiting to be discovered in other far-flung countries!

Anyway, after dinner we went up to our habitual haunt in the Nook, and with the music on and the smooth vanilla musk of a scented candle filling the air, I showed Nick the photos I'd taken. He laughed at the picture of the old-fashioned man which had ended up in my collection by mistake, but he suddenly paused.
"That's weird" he said very quietly. I hadn't heard him sound so worried before.
"What?"
"This picture. There's something really strange about it. This was taken in the same place we were yesterday, at the old mill. The same spot where you were taking photos too."

I leaned over, realising I hadn't really looked at it properly before.
"Yeah, I see what you mean" I agreed. "That's a coincidence"

"I don't think it's a coincidence, Molly" he frowned. "Look there at the edge", he pointed.
"Recognise that? It's my shoe. I was standing in front and to the side of you a bit. You must have taken this.

We were there."

I peered at the photo and my body suddenly felt very cold as I saw he was right.
"How's that possible?" I tried to shake off the icy fingers of fear that were gripping me. "There was nobody else there yesterday".
"It must be a ghost" Nick stated, surprisingly matter-of-fact.

My face must have turned as white as a sheet because I almost *felt* my blood draining away.
"You're very calm about it" I remarked, trying to cover up my own unease. "Only yesterday you barely believed in witches."
He gave a wry smile.
"You learn something new every day" he shrugged. "Besides, I'm still sort of hoping all of this might just be a bad dream and I'll wake up in Islington."

I snorted, breaking the spell and lightening the mood a little. I stared at the photo, wishing it would reveal its secret.

"It looks a bit like an 18th century smuggler or highwayman" I was still a bit spooked. "I suppose I did think when I first saw it that it was overexposed or something, as it looks like he's not quite there. D'you think that's what ghosts really look like?"

It might seem odd that I was so shocked, but even though I'm used to the 'supernatural' when it comes to witchcraft, I had never seen anything like this before. To tell the truth, I'd never really believed in ghosts and I've never been actively involved in witchcraft myself. Mum has taught me lots of things, but it's all about the earth, gardening, herbs and crystals, never any actual spells or anything like that. She always said she wouldn't let me join in until I was older, and only then if I wanted to. I'd grown up with it, so it felt natural, but this was something different entirely.

Maybe I was also on edge after reading about these dark forces that Gerald Gardner had warned my gran and Lawrence about. There was something sinister, dark enough to have killed the old Post Office lady, and a Shakespeare quote sprang to mind – we studied Hamlet last year - "There are more things in heaven and earth, Horatio, than are dreamt of in your philosophy".

Suppressing a shudder, I continued looking at the photo, unable to break away.

"Maybe it's the ghost of that smuggler you mentioned the other day – what was his name?" Nick asked.
"Jeremiah" I responded thoughtfully. I've heard enough stories about ghosts but like I said, I never *really* believed them.
"What do you think he appeared for, then?" Nick continued. "If we HAVE really just captured a ghost on film, don't they usually appear for a reason?"

I pressed my lips together in a firm line and met his eyes solemnly.
"There's something I didn't mention when I first told you the story" I said gravely.

“Jeremiah is meant to appear to people who are in grave danger”.

Nick swallowed. “I feel like my hair’s standing on end. How could we be in danger? It doesn’t make any sense.”

“Let’s put it away” I urged him, tucking it back into the photograph pouch and putting it out of sight in a drawer.

“Why don’t we think about something else?” he suggested. “Tell me another story – not smugglers this time, and definitely no ghosts. Didn’t you say something about a dragon in Burley?”

I was grateful to him for changing the subject, and launched into the tale in an attempt to distract us, although the thought of Jeremiah and his chilling unspecified warning never strayed far from my mind.

“Well, hundreds of years ago, back in the 1400s or so, a dragon terrorised the New Forest. Its lair was at Burley Beacon, just outside the village, but every morning it flew to nearby Bisterne where the villagers would supply it with milk. If they refused, it would carry one of them away, flying back to its lair clutching them in its fearsome claws as they screamed with all their might. They would never be seen again.”

“Riiight. Really believable. So what did they do about it, just wait to get picked off one by one?”

"At first they carried on giving the dragon milk every day. But soon, the villagers began to tire of the arrangement and grew frustrated by the monster's demands," I continued, in my best dramatic storyteller voice.
"The dragon was becoming greedy and demanding more and more, so the farmers were going hungry themselves as there wasn't enough to go around. So one day, a brave man named Sir Maurice Berkeley, lord of the manor of Bisterne, decided enough was enough. He lay in wait with a pack of dogs, and when the dragon arrived they bounded towards it, barking and snapping in a cacophonous din."

"Cacopho-what?"
"Oh, for goodness sake!" I snapped. "Buy a dictionary and stop interrupting my stories!"
"This is coming from the girl who thinks you play 'Blue Lightning' on an Atari *Jaguar*"
"That's totally different! That's not about knowing what words mean, it's about stupid computer games."
"They're not stupid. I still don't know what you spend your time on around here anyway, finding that diary was probably the event of the century for you"
I refused to rise to it.
"I like to read and take pictures" I said patiently. "And creative writing. Which reminds me, you're going to help me write all this down into a proper book, when we eventually find out what happened in 1940."
"I am?"
"Yup. What else is there for you to do, anyway? Like you said, you can't play your silly I'm-pretending-to-be-a-military-pilot game anymore"

"Oh, get on and tell me the rest of this dragon story, then" he said with a sigh.

"Finally, thank you. While the dragon was distracted by the dogs, Sir Maurice was able to attack. There had been attempts before, all ending tragically, but he had planned carefully. Wearing an ordinary suit of armour, the dragon would simply have been able to cut through it with its gigantic claws, like a tin opener, so he covered his armour with glass so it couldn't be penetrated. Sir Maurice successfully slayed the beast, and the villagers were never bothered by dragons again".

"Dragons didn't ever really exist though, did they?" Nick asked. "But then why do they always pop up so much in English folklore?"

I shrugged. "Maybe there was some kind of creature that was unknown to them at the time, and over years and years of re-telling the story, it morphed into the dragons we read about. Some people think the Burley dragon was probably just an oversized wild boar, and the stories of fighting it have been blown way out of proportion over time. Campfire tales."

"Like the Roswell incident in the '50s, when everyone thought there had been a UFO crash, but actually it was probably a weather balloon?"

"Yeah, something like that. Stories and sightings which are exaggerated but in reality can be easily explained."

"Seems a shame, really," Nick said, lost in thought, "if all these stories really just had a logical explanation after all. Talking of logical explanations, can I see that weird photo again?"

"If you want" I gestured towards the drawer where I'd stashed them, having no desire to go near it again myself.

I should have got up to fetch it myself, because Nick demonstrated his characteristic clumsiness and tripped over the same loose floorboard as last time. He circled his arms like a windmill and I cringed as he swept another set of boxes onto the floor with a resounding thud. He managed not to land on the floor but did a funny sort of two-step dance and straightened himself up again at the other end of the attic.
"Have you quite finished?" I said with mock solemnity.
"You need to get that damned floorboard fixed, this place is a death trap!"
"I never have any trouble with it"
"Good for you" he grumbled.
"Right, let's pick it all up then" I said, making my way towards the scattered items. "Last time, we found my gran's diary. I'm looking forward to seeing what you've unearthed for us this time"

He ignored me and started picking up books and papers and cramming them back into their boxes.
I suppose mum and I really should have cleared through all the junk before, but then it takes away all the fun of stumbling across things by accident.

And ‘stumbling’ really is the appropriate word, in Nick’s case.

There didn’t seem to be much of interest this time. I picked up a black leather-bound album hoping it would be old photos, but it turned out to be a stamp collection. I did remember my gran mentioning her stamps once or twice, and she’d been quite interested in them when she was younger. I flipped through, noticing how they had all been very neatly affixed in poker-straight lines, in such perfect condition that I wouldn’t have believed how old they were. Gran had obviously taken this very seriously. Most of them seemed to be from India, but there were a few from other countries.
“I never understood why people collect stamps” Nick commented. “It looks boring to me”
For once, I agreed with him. But one page did catch my eye. It had German lettering along the top along with a couple of black swastikas, and four rows of stamps beneath.
“Der Fuhrer…hat uns…befreit” I struggled, sounding out the words. “Any idea what that means? I chose to do Spanish this year”
“I’m doing German” Nick said. “You completely butchered the pronunciation, but I think it means ‘the Fuhrer has saved us’. So ’Hitler has saved us’ or ‘come to our rescue’ or something along those lines”
I looked more closely and saw that each specimen had actually been stamped. I made out the words ‘Danzig, 1st September 1939’ and gasped.
“Oh wow. Do you know why these are special?” I said.
“No, why?”

"1st September 1939. That means these were stamped on the day that the Second World War broke out. These are probably very rare."
"Better keep them safe then. They might be worth a lot one day."
"Yeah, you're right."
"Did you know Hitler was into the occult?" Nick asked as I gave the pages a final thumb through.
"No, what do you mean?"
"He believed in witchcraft. UFO's too."
"Really? I never heard that before, how do you know?"
"I saw a documentary about it a few weeks ago."

I looked at him with new found admiration.
"You? Watching documentaries?" I asked.
"I'm not just a pretty face you know"
"Ha! I DEFINITELY never said that"
"Yeah, yeah. Anyway, he believed in them so much that he wanted to outdo them. There's a rumour that he was doing experimental aircraft designs and built some kind of hovering flying saucer. It looked really cool. Well, you know, apart from the fact he was a murderer and a dictator and everything, which kind of spoils it"
"So do you like learning about that sort of thing? UFO's? You mentioned Roswell too"
"Sort of. I do like sci-fi and conspiracy theories, but it's more the science behind it that I find interesting, the way these things would have been built."
"You're very clever" I said, really meaning it. "I can never understand that stuff"

"Then we're a good team. You're the witchcraft and history buff as well as the word-master. I'm the science man with a few words of German thrown in. Plus I provide the humour. And the good looks."
I raised my eyebrows.
"And the ability to trip over absolutely anything, thereby uncovering all the clues" I quipped.
"See? Total dream team."

I placed the stamp album reverently back into its box and turned to the other items still strewn across the floor. I recognised my gran's old flute in its case and I tucked it away safely, wishing I had the musical talent to pick it up and play. The rest of the paperwork was boring, but hidden underneath the pile was a framed picture. I studied it carefully, wiping a thin layer of dust away with my finger.
At first I thought it was a photograph, but I was shocked to realise that it was an incredibly realistic colour pencil drawing of a tiger walking through the undergrowth while colourful birds flew overhead. The artist had obviously been very talented. Although it must have been old, the orange was still vivid and the detail of individual hairs and muscle tone made it look as though the animal might come alive and jump out of the frame at any minute.

"Look at this" I said.
"Wow" Nick breathed. "That's amazing. Who drew that?"
"I don't know, but it definitely wasn't gran. The best she could manage was a stick man"

“She must have been interested in India. There were those stamps, and now this picture”
“Mm. I think she did say something about an uncle in the army who was posted there for a while, so maybe that’s why.”
“Why don’t you keep this out and put it on the wall somewhere?”
“I think I will. It’s much too good to keep hidden in a dusty old box.”

We finished packing away the other bits and pieces, and then remembered what Clumsy-Clogs had stood up for in the first place – the spooky photo. He picked up the pouch and flicked through, his eyebrows knitting together. He made a noise of surprise, then started from the beginning of the pack again.
“It’s not here” he said eventually.
“Well I definitely put it back”
“Maybe it fell out? It’s not – oh, hang on. What the - ?”

He gawped open-mouthed. My heart beat faster as my mind raced, wondering what on earth he had seen. I scrambled up and rushed over to have a look, and *I* nearly fell over with astonishment this time. He had found the photo alright, it was definitely the same one because the scene was the same and his foot was still in the righthand corner. But the ghostly man had gone.

And then the lights went out.

I screamed. I'm not normally jumpy or scared of the dark, honestly, but what with the man in the picture being there one minute and not the next, I was terrified. In fact, I'm pretty sure Nick was screaming too even though he denied it later. I felt a rising panic as the darkness swallowed us, that sudden absence of noise and light as everything electrical switched itself off and plunged us into pitch blackness so absolute that the silence rang in our ears and I felt the pressure building in my chest like something was holding me down and I couldn't get away. Instinctively I tried to run, but stumbled and fell headlong onto the floor with a crash, my breath coming in sharp gasps. Nick brushed against me and I nearly screamed again. Turning, I realised there was still a teeny tiny pinprick of wavering light coming from the candle I had lit earlier, although it did nothing to alleviate the darkness. Using the glint to orient myself, I scrambled towards it knowing that it would lead me closer to the door. I scraped my hand against a sharp corner of a chest but didn't even feel the pain.

Suddenly, the lights came back on, making me shield my eyes in surprise. I picked myself up from the floor and dusted myself off. I think we were both a bit embarrassed by our panic.

"What's going on up there?" shouted mum. Opening the door and running downstairs, Nick following closely on my heels, I called out, "Power cut! Didn't you even notice?"

"No" she shook her head, confused. "We didn't have a power cut, the lights have been on down here the whole time."

Nick and I looked at each other, fear and foreboding in our eyes.

When we apprehensively returned to the attic a few moments later, we realised the cassette player had turned itself on again after the 'power cut' too, but it was stuck. Joan Jett was just starting to sing 'Have you ever seen the rain' and I shivered again as it jittered and warped.
"There's a calm before the st-st-st-storm I know, and it's been coming for some ti-ti-ti-ti-time".

I switched it off at the plug and we spent the rest of the evening in the living room watching Disney's Bedknobs and Broomsticks with mum to take our minds off what had happened, but the story drew an uncanny parallel with the events in my gran's diary – evacuated children helping a witch to thwart a German invasion. After Nick went back next door, I found myself drifting off to sleep on the sofa and had strange, disjointed dreams of Gerald Gardner flying through the sky on a broomstick, U-Boats landing on the coast and soldiers running through Burley, and policemen finding bodies in the woods. And through it all, I kept seeing and hearing my gran as a young girl calling out in pain, and I didn't know why.

Chapter 9

1940

The following days dragged by in unending monotony as Lawrence and Rachel waited for news from Gerald Gardner about the ritual they had reluctantly agreed to take part in. They passed their time disinterestedly, going through their daily motions on an automatic pilot. Sometimes it even felt like they had imagined the whole thing; indeed the idea of witchcraft and evil forces seemed unreal during the long, hot days when they had to squint against the bright sunlight and gulp lemonade, perspiring and panting in the sultry temperatures that had risen to a fever pitch. Anyone on the outside might have thought it was just an ordinary July day, but Lawrence and Rachel could sense that the air was thick with tension coiled like a spring. They found themselves frequently irritable and impatient, snapping at each other in frustration. Fortunately, Mrs Fernley didn't seem to notice, or if she did, she must have put it down to the bothersome heat and boredom. Neither of them had received letters from home for a while and were anxious for news, but they had to accept that the postal service couldn't always be reliable in wartime. They felt cut off and isolated, their only contact with the outside world being the BBC news broadcasts that Mrs Fernley continued to listen to on the radio each evening.

One evening, Rachel was passing Lawrence's bedroom on her way downstairs for a glass of water when she heard a strange noise, like someone catching their breath. She pressed her ear to the door and listened, and was shocked to hear muffled sobs. She gently pushed the door open and peered around. Lawrence lay curled up on the bed facing the window, clutching his pillow and crying quietly. Rachel paused, unsure of what to do. She wanted to go in and talk to him, but she didn't know what to say and knew he would be embarrassed that she had seen him like this. She suspected he was still missing home and felt sorry for him; she sometimes felt like hiding away and crying too. After thinking for a moment, she silently tiptoed away. She had an idea.

The next morning after breakfast, she slipped out of the cottage clutching her postal order without telling Lawrence where she was going. An hour later, she found him sitting in the garden looking morose.
"Where've you been?" he asked gloomily. "I've been sitting here with nothing to do and nobody to speak to."
"I think you'll be pleased when you see what I've been doing" Rachel grinned, her hands clutching something behind her back. "Close your eyes" she commanded.
"What for? I'm not playing silly games"
"Just close them, you fathead, and put out your hands"

Lawrence opened his eyes to see a brand new sketchbook and set of pens in front of him.
"What… how?" he gasped, eyes lighting up.

Rachel just smiled and didn't answer.
"You… got these for me?" he asked uncertainly.
Rachel nodded. "I remembered what you said about leaving yours behind. I saw this in the village and thought you'd like it"
"Like it? It's champion!" Lawrence beamed. "Thank you. This is perfect!"
It looked like he almost had tears in his eyes.
"It's nothing, don't make a fuss over it" Rachel said, feeling embarrassed. "But you haven't an excuse to be grumpy anymore now."

The sketchbook marked the start of a friendlier chapter for them both, and a more optimistic one for Lawrence. While they waited anxiously for news about the ritual, he spent hours drawing happily in the garden. His favourites were seascapes; pictures of stately yachts with colourful sails set against an azure blue sky dotted with the shapes of distant birds.
"That's really good!" Rachel said, peering over his shoulder one afternoon. "Where did you learn to draw like that?"
He blushed and shrugged his shoulders.
"It's just practice. I've always liked art. You see this one? Those birds in the sky?"
"Yes, seagulls, aren't they?"
"Yes they are. I like to add birds into all my pictures because I sometimes wish I could be like them, soaring free above everything. They don't have to worry about stupid wars and being evacuated, they can go wherever they want to."
His cheeks reddened again as he realised how much he had said. Rachel sat down on the grass next to him and crossed her legs.

"I know what you mean" she said thoughtfully. "It'd be nice to just fly away when you didn't like something. Lucky birds."
"What do you like to do, anyway?" Lawrence asked after a moment, realising he had never really asked.
"You know I like to draw. What's your favourite thing?"
"Oh, this and that. I'm not as good at anything as you are, but I like music. I have a flute at home, but I had to leave that behind. I collect stamps as well"
"Really?" Lawrence said, surprised. He would never have thought the energetic, vibrant Rachel would be the sort to sit quietly and look at stamps. He also felt a stab of remorse that he hadn't troubled himself to ask about her life before; he had been engrossed with his own sadness and was now so happy to be able to draw pictures again that he had never realised Rachel had also left something at home that mattered to her.
"Yes, but not just any old stamps" she explained. "I like to collect the Indian ones because of my Uncle Harold."
"Oh, because he was stationed there? He was killed the other week in Norway, wasn't he?"
Rachel nodded.
"I'm sorry" he said, bowing his head.
"He used to bring stamps home from India for me and told me so many stories. He even gave me a Scinde Dawk, one of the very first from 1852. Don't know how he got his hands on that one, it's worth a lot apparently"
"He sounds like a smashing sort of uncle"
"He was. Did you know, before they used postal stamps in India, they used to have runners who carried letters from one village to another?

They were often attacked by bandits or wild animals. The Mongolian Empire did it better under Gengis Khan actually, they set up a proper system with people riding horses to carry the mail, with posts every so often where they could change over horses."
"You know an awful lot of history" Lawrence said with admiration. "I wouldn't have thought you were so interested in it, you're always so…" he trailed off.
"Talkative?"
"Um, yes. That's it"
She giggled. "It's alright, I know. Back at school I was always in trouble for talking too much. Feels like forever ago, now. I just wish something would happen, there's just nothing to do while we wait. We can't even start collecting acorns for the war effort yet until the autumn."
"What good will acorns do for the war?"
"Mrs Fernley said the soldiers want children to gather as many as possible, because they can be used to make shells for guns".

They had both long since given up the hope that they would be back home before the school term started; the war news seemed to get gloomier by the day and it was now clear that it wouldn't be over any time soon, even if Operation Cone of Power was successful.
The hours ticked by painfully slowly, moods prickly in the heavy heat despite their new-found friendship.

Neither of them had mentioned the ghostly apparition they had witnessed.

Lawrence and Rachel kept it at the back of their minds like a horrifying secret that they would sometimes take out and examine, before hurriedly replacing it in the recesses of their consciousness. It was too much to take in with their worries about the upcoming ritual, and Mrs Fernley had studiously avoided mentioning it too. Knowing her pragmatism, she probably believed, much like Ebenezer Scrooge, that the manifestation was the result of an overstrained digestive system caused by a tough piece of wartime Spam.

One evening over dinner, she surprised them by asking about their families. Although she was still aloof, she had softened towards the children a little in recent days. As a break from the tedium, they were eager to please.
"My mother works in a munitions factory now, and my father is an office clerk but has just joined the Home Guard" Lawrence explained proudly. "I don't have any brothers or sisters. We've always lived in Portsmouth in the same house for as long as I can remember, at the end of a terrace. I've a few aunts and uncles in various places so when we have enough money we go to visit them, so I've seen parts of the New Forest before. I like it when we go to the coast and see the boats bobbing along, and we once went to see the castle at Calshot. I'd love to learn how to sail one day and pilot one of those boats myself".

"How about you, Rachel?" Mrs Fernley asked as she cleared away the cutlery. "Is your father fighting in the war?"

Rachel looked down at her feet. "Not exactly. He… does something top secret in an office, essential war work, so he can't be called up" she lied. She was proud of her father for standing up for his beliefs and refusing to fight, but she didn't know what Mrs Fernley or Lawrence's reaction would be, and she didn't think she could bear to see the disapproval or pity in their eyes if she explained that he was a conscientious objector.
"My mother doesn't work at the moment but she may find a job soon, to do her bit for the war effort" she continued. "Since my uncle died she's been looking after my aunt and their children. My aunt is my father's sister though, I don't know anything about mother's real family. She was adopted, you see. I don't think she even knows who her real parents were."

Mrs Fernley looked up sharply. "Adopted, you say? What a terrible shame"

Rachel was taken aback at the reaction, and relieved that she had decided not to mention her father's pacifism if Mrs Fernley reacted so strongly to things of which she disapproved.
"It's not that bad" Rachel replied, a little defensively. "She always tells me she had a happy childhood with her adopted parents. I call them Grandma and Grandpa because that's what they've always been to me, so it doesn't matter."

An inscrutable look crossed Mrs Fernley's face and her demeanour changed as she clattered with the plates.

"Why don't you go and play outside while it's still light instead of making a nuisance of yourselves in here?" she barked.

Having grown used to Mrs Fernley's caprices of temper, Lawrence and Rachel thought no more of the exchange. It was still unbearably hot and they lay on the grass wishing for a breeze to provide some relief from the oppressive temperatures. Suddenly, the sky seemed to take on a greyish hue and the setting sun all but disappeared over the horizon. Within moments, scudding clouds dotted the heavens and then the first splash of rain came. Big, round drops began to fall and Lawrence quickly pulled himself up, intending to head indoors before they got drenched.
"Wait! Stay!" Rachel shouted, leaning back and tilting her face skyward, sticking out her tongue to taste the long-awaited rain.
Lawrence crossed his arms over his chest and looked uncomfortable as his hair quickly became plastered to his forehead and raindrops dripped off the end of his nose.

He jumped as there was a flash of lightning followed closely by a crack of thunder; not a quiet distant rumbling but a loud, violent clash that must have been almost directly overhead.

Rachel was standing with arms outstretched, spinning around in circles, laughing and smiling as the rain soaked her to the skin.

"Come and feel it!" she called to Lawrence, who was sheltering as close to the house as possible and wishing Rachel would stop being so ridiculous and come indoors.

"Don't be silly, you're getting soaked!" he yelled back, forced to raise his voice over the sound of the intensifying rain pelting the ground like soldiers' boots.

Rachel ignored him and continued her exuberant pirouette, relishing the change of atmosphere and the sensation of the cooling water on her face and hair. It was a euphoric release after days of being stifled, unable to breathe or sleep comfortably, combined with the wire-taut impatient wait for news from Gerald Gardner, the anxiety thrumming unspoken beneath the surface.

Suddenly, she seemed to stumble and then fell sideways, landing on the saturated grass. Just at that moment, a bolt of vertical lightning flashed from the sky and struck the ground where she had been standing just a second earlier.

"Rachel!" Lawrence shouted, running towards her. She seemed confused and stared around with wild eyes as if she were searching for something. He grabbed her arm and hoisted her up, dragging her towards the house. She continued to glance anxiously from side to side. The smell of scorched grass reached their nostrils.

Mrs Fernley appeared in the doorway, face twisted in annoyance.
"What on *earth* are you two playing at?" she bellowed. "Come in at once! You could catch your death of cold, or be struck by lightning. What would I tell your parents if you were killed? Get changed out of those clothes immediately!"

"S- sorry, Mrs Fernley" Lawrence managed, putting a steadying hand on Rachel's shoulder to propel her indoors; her movements were robotic and she didn't seem fully aware of her surroundings.

Later, when the rain had died down and they were safely wrapped up in warm clothes and drinking cups of cocoa at Mrs Fernley's insistence, Lawrence tried to speak to Rachel. At first she didn't respond and he thought she must have gone quite mad, but just as he had almost given up and was about to go to bed, she suddenly spoke.
"Something saved me, you know" she murmured, staring into the distance.
"What do you mean?" Lawrence asked in surprise. "You were incredibly lucky. Just half a second later or an inch closer and you would have been killed."
"Yes, exactly" Rachel turned to meet his gaze and looked at him intensely. "I wasn't just lucky. I *felt* something push me just before it happened. You saw me fall, didn't you? I didn't trip, I felt… I don't know. It was like a big, strong hand nudging me out of the way."
Lawrence felt a chill run up and down his spine, a sensation he seemed to be feeling all too often since coming to Burley.

"Do you mean… like a ghost? Or like *God* intervening?"

Rachel looked down and her feet.
"I don't know. All I know is what I felt. It was a friendly push; it wasn't trying to hurt me, just to get me out of the way."

"D'you think it could have been something to do with the ghost we saw the other day?" Lawrence gave voice to the experience for the first time. "He said 'beware', so suppose he's a benevolent ghost trying to warn us about something."

"Perhaps" Rachel sounded depleted. "I don't know what to think any more. If he was warning me about the bolt of lightning then everything's alright and he's saved me from being frazzled to a crisp. But I don't think that's what he meant when he said 'beware'. I'm sure he's talking about Operation Cone of Power. And I know you think so too".

Lawrence couldn't contradict her. They didn't discuss the matter further, both lost in their own unsettled thoughts. Rachel's garrulous spark was absent, and for once, Lawrence wished she would pipe up with her usual incessant chatter and hare-brained schemes, reassuring him that everything was alright.

The storm didn't alleviate the humidity as much as they had hoped, or perhaps it was the troubling events of the evening preventing peaceful sleep, but that night Lawrence found himself tossing and turning to find a cool spot on his pillow.

Just as he was thinking about getting up for a glass of water, he froze. His ears pricked up and his hairs stood on end as he sensed danger. He became aware of approaching planes in the distance. Although they were safely evacuated, he was under no illusion that they were entirely protected from the perils of war; the port city of Southampton was only about 20 miles away and was one of the prime targets for air raids; it had already been badly hit by bombs on 20th June, and it was not unheard of for the German planes to miss their mark – surely it was possible they could make a mistake and drop their payloads over the New Forest?

Some of the residents had air raid shelters but most who lived in the very rural parts went about their daily business unconcerned. It wasn't unusual to hear planes overhead but to Lawrence's ears, they sounded louder than normal this time. He propped himself up in bed and listened in alarm as they got closer and closer. He jumped up and went to the window, legs turning to jelly.

"What's going on?" Rachel had appeared pale-faced in the doorway having also heard the ominous thrumming. "Can you see anything?"
"No, not yet" Lawrence whispered, peeking around the edge of the curtain. "But their flight path must be right over us, and it sounds like there are a lot of them. They're definitely German - Messerschmitts I think– you can tell by the sound of the engines."

Mrs Fernley too had been roused from her bed, and she hurried into the room clad in a thin pink dressing gown, hair in rollers. The sight was incongruous and at another time the children might have giggled, but tonight their fear was too great for them to even notice.

They all waited, unwilling to lift the blackout curtain to look even though it was completely dark inside the house anyway. In truth, they were scared of what they might see. The noise had increased to a roaring, rumbling, thumping drone as the planes flew overhead, rattling the windows in their frames. A glass ornament tinkled and vibrated on the chest of drawers. The sound of the planes became unbearably loud and they wouldn't have been able to hear themselves speak over the clamour of engines. Each of them was wondering whether the next thing, and indeed the last thing, they would hear would be the explosion of a bomb. Mrs Fernley put one hand on Rachel's shoulder and her other on Lawrence's in a rare display of silent solidarity as they willed the planes past.

Slowly, slowly they allowed themselves to believe that the noise was getting quieter. They stood for a long time, waiting until the sound of the planes had finally receded into the distance.
Rachel realised she had been holding her breath and let it out with relief. Mrs Fernley quickly took her hands off their shoulders.
"Best go back to bed then" she said briskly, and bustled out of the room.

Lawrence's hands were shaking.
"I thought we were done for" he whispered, letting out a low whistle. "God help the town or city that won't be so lucky tonight."
Neither of them could help but think of their parents in Portsmouth, probably rushing outside to the Anderson shelter at that very moment, at the shrill insistence of the air raid siren.

Just as Rachel turned to make her way back to her room, there was a rustle in the darkness. They both gasped as they felt something brush against them.
"What's that?" Rachel hissed. "Was that you?"

He reached over to the bedside lamp and fumbled hurriedly to switch it on, illuminating the room with a gentle glow.

"No, I wasn't anywhere near you" he replied, eyes darting around the room. "I felt it as well, a breeze or something."

"Well, there's nothing here now" Rachel said, heart still pounding. In their previous lives in Portsmouth, neither of them would have been unduly worried by such an event, perhaps assuming that it was a draft edging through the cracks in the window.
But after the ghostly apparition, the disembodied push which saved Rachel from the lightning, and Gerald Gardner's tales of an evil witch out for revenge, they had become jumpy at the slightest sound or noise.
"Why don't you stay in here tonight?" Lawrence suggested quickly. "I mean, I doubt either of us will be able to sleep now anyway. Perhaps we could just

sit and read a book".

Rachel was inordinately relieved at the suggestion, still jittery from her experience in the storm and unwilling to return to her makeshift bed in the rather dark and overbearing study of Mrs Fernley's late husband. Eventually the books fell from their hands as they nodded off into fitful sleep, so neither of them noticed the lamp flicker as a cool breeze wafted through the room along with a susurrating whisper which sounded like "Don't worry… don't worry…don't worry."

The next morning, Lawrence and Rachel felt slightly more optimistic. The scorching heat had broken a little and they felt fresher at the breakfast table despite the night of disturbed sleep. Mrs Fernley made no reference to the plane scare and it was obvious that things had returned to normal despite last night's unusual display of affection.

"Now, I've noticed that your rooms need tidying" she remarked briskly as they chewed their way through thick, stodgy porridge.
"They need dusting and the furniture should be polished. When I get home today I'd like to see them spick and span, and if you've spare time, you might do the parlour too."

Rachel raised an eyebrow but didn't say anything.
"Yes, of course Mrs Fernley" Lawrence answered dutifully, but their good moods were diminishing already at the thought of spending most of the day

indoors cleaning. Before starting on the housework, Lawrence wanted to finish a picture he had been working on. Something about it had been bothering him and he knew it wasn't quite right but he wasn't sure why.

"Hurry up" Rachel begged. "The sooner we start this cleaning, the sooner we can-" she stopped, startled as her eyes lit on the drawing he was working on.
"That's the woods, isn't it? There's the clearing in the middle, and this is the way back through the trees, when we ran"
"Mm. But there's something I was trying to work out. You remember those green eyes glinting in the darkness?"
"Of course. We still don't know what *that* was"
"Well I've been thinking about it." He fiddled with his pen. "I originally drew the eyes up here," he pointed. "I was trying to recreate the scene. But I don't think that's where they were."
"What do you mean?" asked Rachel. "Does it matter where they were?"
"Yes it does" Lawrence responded slowly. "And I think I've got it."
He picked up a green pen and carefully marked two gleaming eyes amongst the low-lying foliage.
"See? I've put them lower down than I thought. Do you remember now?"
Rachel pondered the picture for a moment.
"Yes, I think you're right. They were really quite close to the ground"
"And do you know what that means?" Lawrence turned triumphantly to face her. "It was a cat!"

"But what about the ghastly noise we heard?" Rachel asked. "That horrid shrieking, wailing cry."
"I wondered that, too" Lawrence replied. "And I'm sure it was actually nothing eerie at all. I've heard it once before, when my parents and I visited my cousins somewhere in the countryside. It was an owl! That's why it sounded like it was coming from the trees above us."

They were equal parts relieved and embarrassed to think that they had been so frightened by a cat's eyes and the hooting of an owl.

"Well done" Rachel said warmly. "You've worked it all out. I didn't guess any of that. So there's nothing to be frightened of in the woods after all."
"Apart from evil spirits trying to kill us, you mean" Lawrence corrected her glumly.

They reluctantly began their cleaning duties.
"When d'you think we'll hear something about you-know-what, anyway?" Rachel asked, sighing as she ineffectually waved a duster around.
She refrained from mentioning last night's incident in the storm, pushing it firmly to the back of her mind. The experience had shaken her, and she was trying her best to pretend it hadn't really happened.

"I'm beginning to hope we never hear about it again" Lawrence replied as he gave the chest of drawers a half-hearted wipe with a cloth. "Maybe they've changed their minds and they're not going ahead with it after all".

"Mm. But those planes last night reminded me how bad things are, with the war I mean. Stuck out here in the country we don't see much of it, but I don't want the Germans to win the war and take over England."

"I suppose not, I just hope nothing happens to us. Don't forget Margery Blackthorn" Lawrence said darkly.

They finished cleaning Lawrence's room and stepped into Mr Fernley's study where Rachel slept.

"Ought we to dust his things?" Lawrence asked doubtfully. "She said we weren't to touch anything, didn't she?"

"Perhaps not" Rachel agreed. "But we should tidy the chest of drawers at least and dust anything that doesn't look personal. You polish that horrid old Mahogany desk and I'll do this side of the room".

They worked quietly for a while, each anticipating the completion of their dull task and the chance to escape outside for some fresh air.

"Hello, what's this?" Lawrence broke the silence.
"What's what? If it's anything of Mr Fernley's, you'd better put it back".
"I'm not entirely sure he *is* Mr Fernley".

Rachel dropped her duster and stepped over to the desk where Lawrence was scrutinising a bent old photograph.

"It was tucked under these papers here, just sticking out. I didn't mean to look but I picked it up to tuck it back into the pile and it caught my eye. Don't you recognise her?"

Rachel tucked her hair behind her ears and inspected the photo. It was creased and mottled but the thin nose and chiselled features of the woman in a wedding dress were unmistakable.
"It's Mrs Fernley!" she exclaimed. "She was actually quite pretty then. Look at all that curly hair!"

"Don't worry about that" Lawrence impatiently waved his hand. "Turn it over and look at what's written there."

She squinted at the copperplate handwriting and deciphered the words, *"Wilhelmina Fernley and Thomas Wetherby on their wedding day, 16th September 1912"*.

Her blood ran cold as thoughts raced through her mind. Thomas Wetherby. The evil witch who was killed in a fight over refusing to go to war! The one who had killed Margery Blackthorn.

Lawrence's face had turned ashen. "It seems Mrs Fernley isn't really Mrs Fernley at all, but Mrs Wetherby."
"Why go back to using her maiden name, though?"
"Maybe after he died, she wanted to distance herself from what happened, so people wouldn't associate her with him. He wasn't very well-liked, Gerald said, and the way he died might have been seen as

shameful in those days. Especially if people knew he was a witch."

Rachel nodded.
"So we're staying with the widow of a man whose evil spirit wants to destroy the coven of witches and stop England winning the war. Well, that's just smashing."

"It does sound bad" Lawrence shuddered, looking around the room edgily as if Thomas Wetherby himself was going to loom up behind them at any moment. "But we don't have any proof that Mrs Weth – Mrs Fernley knows anything about it. Did she even know he practiced witchcraft? I can't imagine her approving of that. She might be a bit unfriendly but I'm sure she's not evil. Not like *him.*"

They studied the photo, absorbing the essence of the man who was once Thomas Wetherby, dressed smartly in his wedding suit and holding his new wife's hand. Despite the poor quality of the picture, they could tell that his small, dark, deep eyes seemed to bore into your very soul – not like Gerald's, which carried a glint of joviality despite their unnerving intensity. They shivered, suddenly feeling very chilly.

"Put it back, I don't like it" Rachel hurriedly stuffed it under the pile of papers and stepped away from the desk. "What should we do?"
Lawrence was dispirited.
"I'm not sure" he chewed his lip. "But this means it's more important than ever that Mrs Fernley doesn't discover the slightest thing about what we're doing."

“D’you think she’d try to stop us?”
“I don’t know, but even if she’s not evil, she probably wouldn’t want us getting involved”
“It explains why she was so short-tempered when I asked her about the war memorial in the village square” Rachel realised. “It brings back bad memories for her.”

“It also explains why this room is so dusty” Lawrence forced a smile. “If he died in 1916 as Gerald told us, it’s been unused for 24 years!”

Rachel giggled, but didn’t feel greatly cheered. She wished Mrs Fernley had got rid of all his things and wiped every trace of Thomas away from the house, and she certainly no longer felt comfortable with the idea of staying in this room.
No wonder she struggled so much to fall asleep at night; she now wondered whether it was less to do with being away from the home she was used to, and more a case of the uneasy atmosphere fostered by the surroundings and musty untouched belongings of a long-dead witch.

“We need to tell Gerald” she decided. “He and the others need to know everything they can if they’re to be successful. And he needs to know who Mrs Fernley really is – if she does turn out to be just as evil as Thomas, then maybe he can protect us somehow”.

Lawrence nodded, calming his nerves and setting his jaw in determination.

“Let’s quickly finish this blasted cleaning, and then I think we’ll take another trip into the woods”.

Chapter 10

1990

For several days after the incident in the attic when Nick and Molly had been plunged into darkness, they had kept a low profile and studiously avoided mentioning the mysterious photo, ghosts, smugglers and witches. On a couple of days, Nick had accompanied his Aunt Clarissa on various shopping trips and a check-up at the vets for three of the cats, while Molly's mum had some time off work and had taken her to Bournemouth beach where they stayed overnight in a Bed and Breakfast.

As they returned to normality for a while, they both found the memories of the other night fading and took pleasure in enjoying the summer without too many thoughts of the supernatural. Molly's birthday was coming up that week; she would be turning 15. Not one for parties and with few friends anyway, especially as Eliza was still in Mongolia, she was just looking forward to a cake at home and receiving some new books she had been wanting to read.

Nick had slowly been settling into Burley and feeling more at home, but still missed the old apartment in London and yearned for the hustle and bustle of the city. He could understand now why people enjoyed the countryside, but still wasn't enamoured with the thought of living here permanently.

He missed his old friends too, but he had never been very sociable anyway, preferring instead to play his computer games or while away the hours listening to music while he people-watched from the balcony, imagining the lives and stories of the individuals swept up in those swathes of humanity.

He missed going to the cinema and he missed being able to run to the nearest shop in five minutes if he felt like getting some chocolate or crisps. He missed going to sleep with the constant murmur of traffic in the background, and he even missed the sound of sirens – at least they made you realise you were alive and in the thick of things, whereas in a quiet village you could feel like you didn't really exist because the air sat stale and silent around you and the clock would move so slowly with its laboured *Tick. Tock. Tick. Tock.*

Sometimes the uneventful summer afternoons would make him think of doctors' waiting rooms where the back of your legs stuck to the sweaty sofa leather and you were desperate for them to hurry up and see you so you could go home and have a cold drink, but you were stuck there, just waiting in the treacle-thick atmosphere.

But there were positive aspects, he realised as he mulled over it one night after his aunt's cats had quietened down and she had packed away that loathsome harp. It wasn't a bad place sometimes and he'd hopefully meet some more new people when he started school; besides, he had Molly now whom he already considered a close friend, and her mum had been very welcoming too.

This witchcraft thing was alright, he supposed. He would never have even considered such things before coming here, but he had to admit that he enjoyed Molly's stories and the folklore about dragons and smugglers. He had been shaken by the ghostly picture and the sudden power cut, and try as he might to forget them, the events still circulated in his mind as he tried to reason them out. He wished that his aunt would tell him more about Rachel Morgan and what had happened here during the war. He supposed there must have been a good reason for her reticence, but it piqued his curiosity and he wondered what this Gerald Gardner had got Rachel and her fellow evacuee Lawrence into.

As he pondered for the hundredth time about what had really happened in 1940, he studied the small birthday present he had chosen for Molly yesterday when shopping with Aunt Clarissa. While she stocked up on cat food and staggered up and down Ringwood high street clutching a tartan blanket, a penny whistle and a pack of pink toothbrushes, he had been scouting the ornament and trinket shops in hope of finding something Molly would like. He had settled on a small pewter amulet shaped like a lion, for her Zodiac sign Leo. The lion's eye was a very small ruby; the July birthstone – the shopkeeper had explained that it was only the size of a tiny pinprick since rubies are so expensive, but even so, it should carry its properties and protect the wearer. It came with a small information card written in a looping script, which read:

"Ruby is fiery and captivating; a truly noble stone. Throughout the ages it has been a talisman of prosperity and protection and was used to ward off pestilence and plagues in ancient times. It stimulates the base chakra, increasing energy throughout the body and spirit, as well as promoting a clear mind, wisdom, concentration, motivation and power."

Nick wasn't so sure he believed it himself, but he knew it was just Molly's sort of thing. Turning it over in his fingers meditatively, he felt his thoughts drawn once more to the story of Rachel and Lawrence during the war and felt desperate to know what had happened. Suddenly a germ of an idea planted itself in his mind. Molly's mother obviously didn't know anything else about it, and Aunt Clarissa wasn't willing to say anything, so who else could tell the story? They should track down Lawrence if he was still alive! He was the only other person who would know the full truth about what happened in 1940. With a satisfied smile, he slipped the amulet in his pocket and went next door to join the birthday celebrations.

1990
Molly

I had gone for a walk that morning to pick up some freshly developed photos that I had taken when mum and I were in Bournemouth, and when I got home I found her sitting in the kitchen with Nick, whispering conspiratorially over a huge chocolate cake.

"Happy Birthday!" mum danced towards me wearing a ludicrous party hat.
"Thanks" I smiled, feeling grateful that at least they hadn't invited the whole village. Just then, Aunt Clarissa hove into view and I kept a smile plastered on my face to be polite.

"Many happy returns of the day" she trilled, presenting me with a bowl of trifle.
"Home-made" she clarified proudly.
"Oh, thank you very much, Miss Clutterbuck" I responded, inviting her to sit down and have a piece of cake.
"I'll have a dollop of trifle with it" she winked cheerfully.

While mum served up the cake for our little party, Nick handed me his present – a beautiful Leo amulet with a ruby eye. I was really touched that he had got me anything at all, especially something so very *me*. I was gratified to notice he had even swapped his tatty sweater for a black t-shirt for the occasion, although I expect it had more to do with the rising temperature than anything else.

It was a fun afternoon and we all made ourselves feel pleasingly sick with chocolate cake. I have to admit that even Mrs Clutterbuck's trifle tasted very good, even if I did spot something that looked suspiciously like cat hair in the custard.

Once she had gone back next door and mum had started the clean-up operation, Nick and I went back up to the attic again, where we seemed to spend more time than anywhere else. Most of the eerie feelings had worn off after the mysterious power cut, but I still didn't feel quite as relaxed in there as I used to. I tried my best to shake it off and we distracted ourselves with chatter about my gran's diary.

Nick had come up with a surprisingly good idea, which was to try and trace the mysterious Lawrence and see if he or his relatives remembered anything about the strange wartime events.
"He might not even live in this country anymore" I warned him, "let alone anywhere nearby. And if he's already dead, I doubt we'd find any of his family willing to talk to us if they even know anything about it themselves."

I fiddled with the Leo amulet in my pocket, finding that it helped me think. We'd been trying to work out how we could possibly track Lawrence down without so much as a surname when it suddenly came to me.
"The vicar!" I cried out.
Nick looked at me oddly.
"The vicar? What are you talking about?"

"Do you remember at the beginning of my gran's diary, she explained that the vicar was in charge of organising which evacuee went to which home? He met them at the station with a list."

His eyes lit up in understanding.
"Oh, I see what you mean" he said, flipping his hair for the umpteenth time. "What if he kept all the records somewhere in the church or vicarage? It could still be there! But there've probably been lots of different vicars since 1940, so I doubt they would have kept all those old papers."

"But it's worth a try" I pressed. "Reverend Bumble is our vicar at the moment and he's very friendly, if a bit mad. But we'll have to tell him a cover story. We'd better not mention Lawrence by name in case he's heard stories about what happened. Don't forget he's religious and wouldn't want anything to do with witchcraft. We'd better tell him we're researching the war for a school project over the summer."
"Alright, good idea. But don't forget even if we manage to find his name, we'll still have to work out how to track him down now, fifty years on."

Invigorated by our plan, I waved aside Nick's concerns. We'd worry about that later – for now, we had a visit to make.

We wasted no time in heading out straight away and considered it more likely that the Reverend would be in the church at this time of day than his vicarage home.

Not a place I normally frequented, I'd nevertheless always savoured the smell and feel of churches. Stepping inside meant walking into a different world, where the noise and heat and buzz of everyday life is suddenly muffled and you're surrounded by a feeling of stillness and peace. The saints endlessly peer up to heaven in their stained-glass worlds as though nothing else exists, and the faint smell of musty books makes it feel like you're in a museum. Closing the door gently behind us and feeling the relief of the cool air inside, we blinked as our eyes adjusted to the dim lighting after the brightness of the sun outside. Dust motes danced in the air, illuminated by the few columns of light that had managed to battle their way through the windows and we spotted Reverend Bumble shuffling papers at the pulpit. As we walked closer he glanced up and greeted us.

"Hello, young people!" he smiled amicably, always ready with a laugh and a joke. "Have you come to have a word with Jesus? Or are you just seeking some respite from the beating sun?"

"Hello, Reverend Bumble" I greeted him cheerfully. "We were wondering if you could help us. We've been set a summer research project for school, for our GCSE History. It's about how Burley was affected by the Second World War, and we want to know how many evacuees were sent here and what their lives might have been like."
"Oh, delightful, delightful! How can I help?"
"We found out that the vicar here at the time organised everything, and we thought maybe there might be some records here still."

“Hmm” he scratched his salt-and-pepper beard and furrowed his brow. “Maybe. Good to see you kids keeping out of trouble!” his lips twitched. “Anyway, I need to prepare for evening worship in a minute but I can have a quick look in the vestry for you. In the meantime, make yourselves comfortable and pull up a pew”. He chuckled to himself at his own joke.

We perched stiffly on the hard wooden benches and waited, hoping against hope that he would find something – if not, we had no idea where else we could possibly look. We held our breath as he emerged from the back room clutching a wad of papers and whistling a jaunty sea shanty to which I imagined the lyrics were far from holy.

“You’re in luck!” he beamed, rustling the stack of files. “I found them tucked away with all the other parish records. They’re a bit old and musty, mind, but let’s see if there’s something useful in here.”

We peered over his shoulder, struggling to read the curling, old-fashioned script.

“1939, 1940… ah, here’s something” Reverend Bumble muttered. “The vicar here during the war was Rev. Chalkford. It looks like the evacuees started arriving in the summer of 1940. What do we have here… Eleanor Brown, Julie Thomas, John and Peter Morris… quite a lot of names, and in no particular order. It doesn’t say much else though, so I’m not sure how useful it is to you.”

"It's great" I assured him. "If it ok if we take some notes?"
"Of course, of course. I'm afraid these originals mustn't leave the church though, so you'll have to stay here while you do it."
"That's fine" Nick said. "We'll just sit here for a few minutes."

We thanked him, feeling a bit guilty for not telling the whole truth. We perched on the pew while he busied himself preparing for the next service, and trawled through the names.

"Look at this!" Nick pointed at a scrawled note at the bottom of a list. I slowly deciphered the handwriting.

"Rachel Morgan, aged 12, was put on this train in error and ought to have gone to Blandford Forum. Mrs Fernley of 26 Turnbull Cottages kindly took her in along with her original assigned evacuee Lawrence Longley".

I gasped.
"That's my house!" I whispered. "26 Turnbull Cottages! So our home actually once belonged to Mrs Fernley. How on earth did it come to be my gran's?"

Reverend Bumble had bustled over again on hearing my excitement.
"Found something interesting?" he asked, eyes twinkling.

"Yes, we have" I replied, relieved to be able to tell the truth about something – I suppose we *were* interested in the general history, even if we didn't mention the witchcraft bit, and I was genuinely excited to learn anything I could about my gran.

I told him that she had been evacuated here during the war and that the house she stayed in now belonged to us, her descendants.

"Unusual" the Reverend remarked. "I wonder why she didn't go back to her family after the war? Still, isn't it fascinating to think she only ended up here by a chance mistake? You could have been living somewhere quite different now!"

That thought made me feel odd. It was strange to imagine that I might never have been here at this place and time if everything had gone according to plan in 1940 and Rachel had gone on to Blandford Forum and stayed with a different family and never met Lawrence or Gerald Gardner.

I glanced at Nick, wondering if we should take the chance of explaining more and asking for guidance. I went ahead.
"Reverend, do you have any ideas that could help us? We'd really like to meet one of the evacuees if he's still alive – Lawrence Longley, who was staying in the house with my gran Rachel Morgan."
"Why would you want to do that?" he asked, furrowing his brow.

"I don't know much about gran's childhood and I'd love to speak to someone who knew her when she was young. Do you think there's a way of finding out where he lives now?"

Reverend Bumble scratched his beard and I crossed my fingers hopefully.
"Alright then, let me have another look through that old paperwork, see if there's any clues" he smiled, rustling the yellowing papers. "1943, 1944, 1945…no, nothing there. Oh hold on, there's a note here about which evacuees were sent home and when. Your granny isn't listed here, so she must indeed have stayed. Lawrence, Lawrence, where are you… ah, yes, it says he returned to his family in 1945 safe and sound. I'm afraid there's no further information, but at least you know he survived the war here."

Disappointed but grateful for his help, we thanked the Reverend and headed home, wondering how we could possibly locate Lawrence.

"We could try the phone book" Nick suggested as we walked back through the village.
"There's bound to be more than one Lawrence Longley, though. How would we know which is the right one? Anyway, what would we say? 'Hello, remember your friend Rachel during the war? I'm her granddaughter; please tell me your life story?'"
"Haven't you ever seen the film Terminator?"
"No, what's that got to do with it?"

“He’s looking for a Sarah Connor so he goes through the phone book and even though there’s hundreds, he tries every single one until he finds her. Haven’t you seen *any* good films?”
“We watched Bedknobs and Broomsticks the other day, remember?”

Nick raised an eyebrow in the scathing way I wish I could master myself.
“Um. It might be good if you’re ten years old.”
“Hey! There’s nothing wrong with Disney films. Besides, I don’t remember you complaining at the time. You loved it, really.”
“Whatever. So are we going to do this thing with the phone book or not?”

Although I had rolled my eyes at the suggestion, I had to admit that the idea had promise, and that it might be the only possible way. We still didn’t know whether Lawrence was even alive or whether he’d moved far away or even overseas, but we could at least see how big a task it would be, and establish whether it was a case of trawling through 5 or 50 Lawrence Longleys in the phone book.

Back at home, I turned the kitchen drawers upside down until I found the latest directory, and we thumbed through to the ‘L’ page.

“L-a, L-e, L-i, here are the L-o’s” we skimmed the names and couldn’t believe our luck when we saw there were only three Lawrence Longleys listed.

With a bit of quick thinking, we were able to narrow it down immediately as one of the area codes was a Southampton one which I recognised. We knew he came from Portsmouth originally so it wasn't such a stretch to think he had eventually settled fairly close by.

"Did I hear you say I'm a genius? You're welcome" Nick said, gloating that his idea had worked. I ignored him.

"Here goes then" I said, heart beating faster as I picked up the phone. "Don't fluster me!"
We'd been so sure of what we were doing, that now I felt a bit silly thinking that we could just phone some stranger and start asking him about his wartime experiences and whether he knew my gran. I didn't know what to say, so I stuttered a bit when a man with a gravelly voice answered.

"Hello?"
"Um, hello. My gran – I mean, I, I'm sorry, I'm getting all muddled. Is that Mr Lawrence Longley?"
"Yes, who is this?" was the terse reply.
"My – my name is Molly Morgan. I'm trying to trace my family history and learn more about my gran who was evacuated to Burley during the war."

There was a sharp intake of breath and I knew he was the right one.

"Rachel Morgan" he murmured. "Is she still… alive?"

"I'm sorry, she died seven years ago" I replied. "But she had a daughter called Lilianna, that's my mum. I'm her granddaughter."

There was a silence.
"Well" he sighed. "It was a long time ago. We knew each other well as we were evacuated together, but we lost touch after the war. I live in Calshot now and never went back to Burley. Too many memories."

"I wondered if I could… come and visit you?" I said on the spur of the moment. Nick looked alarmed and raised his eyebrows at me, shaking his head in despair.
"I'd love to know more about her. I found her diary from 1940 you see, and it mentioned you, and… and everything that happened that summer. In the forest."

The moment the words had left my mouth, I knew I'd made a mistake. His tone changed immediately, becoming guarded and suspicious.

"What do you mean, everything that happened that summer? The imagination of a 12 year old child writing a diary. Don't ask me what stories she came up with."

"I – I'm sorry. I just wanted to know what –"

"You shouldn't go digging up the past" he snapped. "Don't call again".

And with that, he put the phone down.

"What was all *that* about?" Nick asked as I replaced the receiver.

I set my mouth in a determined line and said resolutely, "We're going on a trip to Calshot."

Chapter 11

1940

Rachel and Lawrence hurried through the woods, desperately searching for Gerald Gardner's grotto and hoping he would be there. They hadn't any idea of where he actually lived, but assumed he couldn't possibly stay in the grotto *all* the time. The forest had taken on an unfriendly demeanour and once they had left the road behind and Mrs Fernley's cottage was no longer visible, the air seemed to close in on them and the branches of the trees became menacing, looming over them and encompassing them with a darkness that seemed too deep for the sunny afternoon it should have been. The grating screech of a crow reached their ears and they realised that no other birds were chattering and chirping. It was like a warning; a subtle shift towards further danger, a precursor perhaps, of things to come.

"What have you come here for?" a voice hissed behind them, making them spin round, startled. It was Gerald Gardner himself, waving his stick and gesticulating angrily. "I told you to wait for news!"

"Sorry, Mr Gardner" Rachel said. "We were careful and nobody saw us come into the woods, I promise. But we've discovered something you have to know. It's about Thomas Wetherby."

His expression softened and he looked quizzical, gesturing for them to follow him. The little cave was not far away, but once inside the children didn't feel the same sense of calm and forest tranquillity that they had noticed on the first occasion. The woods were unnervingly silent, and something felt off somehow. A couple of moments later, Lawrence realised that it wasn't just the birds that had fallen silent; they could no longer hear the trickling of the nearby stream, and even the frogs and insects had become silent.
"Tense, isn't it?" Gerald coughed, sensing their unease. "It's been like this since yesterday. All coiled up tight like a spring just waiting for release. Who knows if that spring will kick back and hit us all in the face?"

Lawrence and Rachel glanced at each other, beginning to regret their involvement in what was swiftly becoming a living nightmare.
"I was going to send a message to you today, in fact" Gerald continued. "We are going to attempt Operation Cone of Power tonight. 11:30.As luck would have it, we've one less thing to worry about as that chap from Scotland Yard has gone home. Apparently couldn't glean anything; poor Margery's gone down in the books as 'unsolved'. Anyway, what did you want to tell me?"

Lawrence gulped. "Tonight?" he quavered, feeling the panic rising. He knew it had been imminent but had expected a little more warning.

As anxious as they had both felt while waiting for news, it now seemed startlingly real and the enormity of what they were involved with lay heavy on their shoulders.

As they explained the photograph they had found, Gerald's expression darkened.
"Mrs Fernley" he muttered thoughtfully. "I wouldn't have thought it. Wilhelmina with her winning smile and curls. I would never have thought she would have ended up with *him*."
"You knew her?" Rachel asked, surprised.
"Oh yes, in my youth. But later I lived in Christchurch, so I didn't hear that she had married anyone at all, let alone Thomas Wetherby. Of course, as she's going by her maiden name there's no reason I would have known. Although I've seen her around the village a couple of times since, she keeps herself to herself now, as you must have noticed. She never spoke about a husband. I assumed she was only calling herself "Mrs" to put off any would-be suitors, although the way she is now, I don't think she need be worried about that."

He gazed wistfully into the distance.
"She was lovely once, you know" he went on. "Always a sunny disposition. Never cross, never frowning. When I came back to Burley to join the coven I knew she had changed but couldn't work out why – it all makes sense now. Being married to Wetherby would have been enough to wipe the smile off anyone's face, and then his being killed four years later in a pointless fight…well, it doesn't bear thinking about". He shook his head.

"But should we be worried?" Rachel persisted.
"Would Mrs Fernley know about her husband's evil spirit? Would she want to destroy our operation too?"

Gerald thought for a moment.
"I don't believe so" he answered. "After all, the very fact she goes by the name of Fernley and not Wetherby suggests she wants to distance herself from any link to him. She certainly wouldn't do anything to jeopardise the war effort – she's a good woman even if she's bad-tempered these days. She would never betray her country."

"That's what we thought. But she still keeps his study the way it was, though" Lawrence remembered.
"She's got all his things just the way they were and forbids anyone to touch them. Why would she do that?"

"That I can't answer" Gerald tapped his stick on the ground thoughtfully. "But perhaps she does mourn him and their short-lived marriage. We might all have thought badly of him, but she must have seen something in him I suppose."

"We'd better make doubly sure that she doesn't find out what we're up to tonight" Lawrence said.
"Yes, you're right" Gerald agreed. "If she were to find out that Wetherby is the one causing the trouble, there's no telling what effect it might have on her. I imagine you can sneak out tonight with no problems?"

“Well, we’ve done it before” Rachel replied. “We’ll set off early and be at the clearing in good time. Should we bring anything with us?”

“No, just yourselves and your fighting spirit” Gerald’s face split into a rare, wrinkled smile. “Don’t forget the words of the great Bard; ‘Our doubts are traitors, and make us lose the good we oft might win, by fearing to attempt’.”

“He likes his Shakespeare quotes, doesn’t he?” Rachel pulled a face as they made their way back through the woods, in an attempt to lighten the mood as the apprehension about the night ahead hovered vulture-like over their shoulders.

Lawrence didn’t reply, lost in his own fears and wondering how he would summon up the courage to return to the woods that night and take part in a ritual which had already caused the death of one of its participants. He had come out of his shell a great deal since those first days after arriving in Burley, mostly thanks to Rachel’s kindness in giving him the sketchbook and pens.

He no longer wished he had been evacuated anywhere else and was thankful that due to a chance mix-up, they had ended up together. As they were both only children, it was almost like they were the brother and sister that each had never had. Even so, he was still terrified about the ordeal awaiting them that night and he withdrew into himself, keeping his worries private. Rachel on the other hand, was full of nervous energy and couldn’t keep still.

Just as scared as Lawrence, her way of coping was to be as boisterous as possible to try and distract herself from her real feelings.

Mrs Fernley sensed something was up and eyed them both suspiciously a few times that evening, but didn't say anything. She had softened a little in recent days and although she still had a sharp tongue and a semi-permanent scowl, the children were almost convinced that she had developed a small amount of affection for them, and she had solicitously ensured they had a sweet pudding after their dinner every day, in spite of the rationing.

Perhaps she also seemed more human to them since they had seen the old photo of her and now they had heard Gerald describe her as 'lovely' in her youth. Rachel had been worried that she would make good on her promise to speak to the vicar and arrange for her to be shipped off to another billet, but there had been no mention of it since the first day so it seemed that it was forgotten.

They climbed into bed fully-clothed and lay sleeplessly listening to the creaks and groans of the house and Mrs Fernley's movements until gradually the noises fell silent and they were satisfied that she must have finally gone to bed.

The hands on the clock seemed to tick more and more slowly until Lawrence and Rachel were so frustrated that they thought they would scream. Eventually, 11:00 came and it was time to start making their way to the clearing.

Shaking despite the warmth of the summer night, they wordlessly took their torches, put on their outdoor shoes and crept from the house.

As they traversed the woods as quietly as they could, jumping at the occasional snap of a twig or the hooting of an owl, their ears pricked up at the sound of voices in the distance. Adrenaline coursing through their veins, they pushed their way onwards. There was no talk of turning back; the notion was unthinkable. They had agreed to play their part and they would follow it through to the end, terrified or not.
"Think of all the soldiers who give their lives each day in the war" Rachel whispered, sensing Lawrence's fear as well as trying to alleviate her own.
"I know" Lawrence whispered back gratefully. "And think of our classmates killed by bombs".

As they emerged into the clearing, they saw that the others had already begun gathering. There must have been fifty people there, most dressed in robes and some clutching unusual items like the ones they had seen on that night that felt so long ago, when they had made their first foray into the woods. Some were clutching brooms, others sprigs of greenery, one a ceremonial dagger.

They looked around, feeling lost, and recognised some of the local women who had clustered outside the Post Office on the morning that Margery Blackthorn's death had been discovered.

A clear voice rang out and the children were surprised to realise it was Gerald's, his usual gruff tones replaced with a powerful, pure bass.

"You're here!" he said, striding towards them as the crowd of people parted to let him through. He wasn't clutching his stick and he stood erect with no sign of his usual crouched, aged demeanour. The children wondered which was his real appearance; was his 'old man' persona just an act? Or did he somehow regain his youth temporarily each time he performed magic?

Everyone fell silent and Lawrence and Rachel blushed as Gerald introduced them.
"I've told you all about these two brave young people" he announced theatrically. "And here they are. Quite by chance, they find themselves risking life and limb for our country, just like all of you here today. We may only hope that their youthful spirit will add to our own power to create the energy that we need. Now, let Operation Cone of Power begin".

There was a muted bustle as the witches took their places in a circle around a large spitting and crackling fire.

"Don't worry" Gerald whispered to Lawrence and Rachel. "Just join the circle, holding hands with the person either side of you. Ignore the daggers and brooms and robes – mostly they're for show, and some of us are reassured by them."

"But what do we have to do?" Lawrence asked.

"Simply *feel* your energy joining with ours, and wish with all your heart for us to be successful." Gerald explained. "Visualise England's victory. When Patricia says the words, 'Propel the Cone' – " he pointed at a woman dressed all in white, crowned with a halo of twisted green leaves - "just think as hard as you possibly can as if you are talking to the German High Command. Think how dangerous it would be for them to attempt a Channel crossing. Think of discouragement and failure for them. Send those thoughts to them. And whatever you do, whatever happens, do *not* break the circle or drop hands. Do you think you can remember that?"

Lawrence and Rachel nodded numbly, not fully understanding how this was meant to work, but determined to do what they were told. Mr Gardner seemed to think that their presence and thoughts would make a difference, so they would accept his faith in them and try their best.

They held hands and joined the circle. On Rachel's left side was a tall, thin man with a clammy palm and she thought she recognised him from the village shop. Somehow the knowledge that he was also sweaty and nervous did little to steady her nerves.

If even these seasoned witches were scared and anxious about the outcome, how on earth could she and Lawrence hope to be of any help? On Lawrence's right side was one of the women from outside the Post Office who had told them about Margery Blackthorn.

She squeezed his hand and whispered with a jovial smile, “Fancy seeing you here!” He was grateful for it, and felt his panicked heartbeat slowing slightly.

And then all at once, the niceties were over and the group fell silent. The lady called Patricia began pacing around the circle, tall and majestic, sprinkling generous amounts of salt in an unbroken ring. She stepped inside the circle and shook the last of the salt on the ground to close it, before joining hands with those on either side of her.

Then her voice rose like a bell with sparkling, silvery clarity.
“Guardians of the Watchtowers, I call upon you! Air in the East, I invoke you. Fire in the South, I invoke you. Water in the West, I invoke you. Earth in the North, I invoke you. Energies of the above, please protect this circle. Energies of the below, please protect this circle. I call out to the guardian of the sacred centre to protect this circle!”

Lawrence and Rachel weren’t sure what they expected to happen, but they were almost disappointed when the woods remained silent.
After a few moments they began to think it would all be a failure, when they heard a breeze rustling in the trees and felt an aura of solemnity fall over the circle. They gripped each other’s hands more tightly.

The witches began humming a single note, louder and louder until the children felt their eardrums vibrating. On and on the humming went, and then some members of the group began singing.

The words were indecipherable. Lawrence and Rachel didn't know what they were, but they certainly weren't English. The harmonies rose and fell as the background humming continued, and they felt themselves pulled round step by step as the circle of witches began to walk slowly round and round the fire.

Then as suddenly as the singing had begun, it stopped. Patricia began to speak once more.
"We are gathered here for our country. We must harness the energy of these brave souls so we can save lives and put an end to this conflict. As the Wiccan Rede states, we must harm none. Our actions today will not endanger lives, but protect them. Without our efforts, many more will die. I call upon the Goddess to give strength and protection to this sacred circle and to our cause."

She bowed her head and Lawrence and Rachel were astonished to feel energy coursing through their bodies – almost like electricity. As Gerald had instructed, they focused on it and the way their own vital life force mingled with the power of the circle. They visualised victory for England as hard as they could, focusing more than they ever had before.

Rachel almost gasped as images came into her mind unbidden; soldiers dancing in the streets, bunting hanging from windows, and a newspaper bearing the year 1945 and the words 'V.E. DAY'.
A haunting song reached her ears, which sounded just like the singer Vera Lynn, but it was a song she had never heard before.

She focused on the melody as she felt the energy racing through her. The words sounded like "there'll be bluebirds over the White Cliffs of Dover". Her head swum and she thought she might faint, but she clung tightly to the hands of Lawrence and the man to her left, wondering if the others were experiencing the same.

Then the words came.
"Propel the Cone".

They imagined pushing their thoughts towards Germany, straight into the minds of the hated Hitler and the High Command. They summoned up feelings of disaster and terror for any invasion across the Channel. They sent as many discouraging thoughts as they could manage, spurred on by the feelings of victory in their own hearts.

Lawrence trembled as he, too, felt the thrumming, throbbing power flowing from hand to hand around the circle. It was electrifying. He lost all perception of the forest around him, the sense of the ground beneath his feet and the crackling sound of the fire. It was like floating in a bubble and it was like nothing he had ever experienced.

Suddenly pain flooded his body and he jerked his head back in agony. The thoughts and the energy faded and he realised where he was as spasms flooded through him. He looked around in panic and saw the rest of the group were similarly afflicted.

"Don't let go!" Gerald's voice boomed out, but it was too late. Lawrence felt Rachel let go of his left hand and she screamed and tumbled to the ground.
The witches clustered around her, the closest dropping to their knees and lifting her wrist to check her pulse.
Gerald pushed his way through the crowd. They were no longer holding hands; the circle was broken.
"Is she alright?" he barked, bending at her side and studying her for signs of life.
"She's breathing!" Lawrence shouted in relief, knees trembling with fear.

Sure enough, Rachel was breathing faintly. Her eyelids fluttered and Gerald pulled her gently into a sitting position.
"Wh – what happened?" she whispered.
"Thomas Wetherby" Gerald spat. "*That's* what happened. He tried again, but thank the goddess, this attack was not fatal. We must have been a little too strong for him this time."

The night unfolded into a whirlwind of activity of which, when trying to remember it later, Lawrence could only recall dreamlike fragments.
The group had disbanded and Gerald had made the decision that Mrs Fernley should be informed, and Rachel was to be checked over by the doctor.

"It's not just the fact that she needs to know about Rachel's accident" he explained grimly, "but I feel the time has come to explain the Wetherby situation to her. We need her help."

“Help from Mrs Fernley?” Lawrence gaped, feeling stupid.
“I’m afraid so” Gerald explained. “He won’t stop trying to use his evil power to defeat us unless someone can communicate with his spirit and make him understand that his actions are wrong. Wilhelmina is the only one with any chance of doing that. If we don’t even try, more of us may be injured or killed. Rachel is incredibly lucky to be alive.”

“Where’s Wetherby gone now?” Lawrence asked. “Why did he go away after hurting Rachel, why not harm the rest of us?”

“I’m not sure” Gerald admitted. “But I like to think it’s because he doesn’t have unlimited power and can only do so much in one night. He’s got what he wanted for now – he’s interrupted Operation Cone of Power, so I doubt we’ll hear anything more from him until we try again next time”.

Lawrence was horrified at the thought of there being a next time, but his main concern for now was Rachel’s safety. Gerald had lifted her as if she weighed no more than a feather and strode briskly through the forest back to Mrs Fernley’s cottage, his strength again belying his previously frail appearance. During the ritual he had exuded a power and exuberance beyond anything the children could have imagined, and his vitality now seemed like that of a much younger man.
If they hadn’t already believed in witchcraft, Gerald’s transformation would have been proof enough.

Lawrence trotted along behind, trying to keep up a stream of conversation with Rachel to keep her conscious. She was awake but didn't respond much; it was as if all her energy had been sucked out of her.

When Lawrence thought back to how Mrs Fernley had reacted when they had all burst through the front door in the middle of night, spilling out the whole story, he couldn't remember much apart from her understandable shock. She had been surprisingly worried about Rachel's wellbeing, tucking her up on the settee with a blanket around her and lifting her head as she encouraged her to drink a few drops of brandy.

The doctor was called and when he asked how Rachel had been taken ill, he was simply told that she had woken up in the night and complained of feeling sick and dizzy, fainting when she tried to stand up. He inspected her thoroughly and packed away his stethoscope with a puzzled expression.

"Well, Miss Morgan here seems to be well for the most part" he concluded. "She has a racing pulse and is a little feverish but I'm not sure what could have caused it. Fainting is unusual in an otherwise healthy child, but perhaps she's overwrought and distressed about her situation.
Many evacuated children feel anxiety and it could be that she's coming down with something. For now, simply give her plenty of water and good plain food, make sure she rests and call me straight away if she deteriorates or appears nauseous or confused".

Gerald had been hiding upstairs during the doctor's visit to avoid awkward questions being asked about his presence, but hurried down afterwards to hear Mrs Fernley's report with relief. His persona seemed to have reverted to the old, frail one that Lawrence and Rachel were used to, his voice less strident and his frame smaller, weaker. His face was full of guilt and he knew that if he hadn't insisted on the children taking part in the ritual, none of this would have happened. But at the same time, he sensed that they were needed. Without their contribution, the Cone of Power would not work. There was no use in sending word to other local villages to find any other adults who might be willing to take part; for some reason these children were the key. He wrestled with his conscience as he acknowledged that he had forced them to take a terrible risk. It was a miracle that they were still both alive. How could he possibly ask them to go through with it all again?

As if reading his thoughts, Rachel stirred and murmured, "Don't worry, Mr Gardner. I'll be fine, and we'll try again".

Mrs Fernley bristled.
"You will do no such thing. You've nearly been killed once already."

Then, Gerald had seen no choice but to explain that Mrs Fernley herself was also needed. Until then, he had kept the facts brief and merely explained Operation Cone of Power and told her that something had gone wrong.

Aware of the long history of witchcraft in the area, Mrs Fernley was not unduly surprised, although she was terribly disapproving and angry that the children had been involved. But when she was told that it was her long-dead husband whose evil spirit was attempting to foil them and had already killed Margery Blackthorn, her shock was palpable.

Slumping heavily into an armchair, she didn't speak for several minutes, her features showing little but her eyes revealing how deeply troubled she was.
"Thomas?" she asked, shaking her head. "Thomas has done all this? You're telling me his… *spirit* lives on? Why hasn't he shown himself to me? Why on earth should I believe this nonsense?"

Gerald put a hand on her shoulder and gently explained.
"The damage has clearly been done" he pointed at Rachel. "And let's not forget poor Margery. As for why he doesn't communicate with you, well, it doesn't always work like that."
"What do you mean?"
"It's not really *him* as such, just all the dark parts of his soul seething and bubbling, lurking around here on earth. Nobody fully understands it, but this is what we believe. It's doubtful that in this state he would even remember you, I'm afraid. He isn't a full person; he's been reduced to a cloud of evil. And we need your help."

"H-how could I possibly help?" Mrs Fernley stuttered. Lawrence felt himself drawn to sit near her, sensing her distress.

It made him very uncomfortable to see her reduced to this state, having become so familiar with her sharp tone and brackish moods.

"We need you to take part along with us when we make our next attempt at the Cone of Power" Gerald explained, anxiously twirling the stick he clearly didn't always need. "If anyone can reach the small part of him that still understands, it will be you. Your presence might tempt him to reveal himself and the distraction may weaken him, rendering his interference with the ritual less potent."
"But what would I say?"
"Perhaps you could try to make him remember what he used to be and realise what he has become. You may be able to convince him to stop."
"What if he won't?" Mrs Fernley was worried. "He never listened to me much when he was alive, so I doubt my words would mean much to him now." She shook her head. "Am I dreaming? I can't understand how I'm really agreeing to all this."

"Well, we must accept it is a slim chance" Gerald admitted gently. "But it's the only chance we have, so I don't see what we can do except try."

"So you'll let me do it again too?" Rachel exclaimed from her position on the settee, her voice a little stronger.
"You *have* to let us both try. We were so close, I know it!" Lawrence surprised himself with his vehemence.

Mrs Fernley hesitated but Gerald answered for her.

“I’m afraid we must” he sighed. “I don’t wish to put any of you in danger again, but we have no choice. Wilhelmina, you must see how much the children want to take part, despite being so frightened. We must let them. For we all, at some time, are masters of our own fates. The fault, you see, is not in our stars but in ourselves.”

He rose and let himself out, turning only to say, “We meet again tomorrow night at the same time. Be ready.”

Chapter 12

1990

When Molly announced her intention of taking a trip to Calshot to visit Lawrence in person, Nick was shocked. He had already realised his new friend was headstrong to say the least but he hadn't expected the situation to progress so quickly. He almost regretted ever suggesting tracking Lawrence down; in a way he hadn't truly expected to find him. He was still intrigued to discover Molly's grandmother's history and the truth about the events of 1940, but he was concerned about being dragged into an escapade of the sort that he was likely to regret.

"Go and visit?" he said incredulously. "It sounds like he just slammed the phone down on you; I doubt he's going to welcome us with open arms."

Molly flicked her hair over her shoulder with a determined expression.
"It will be harder for him to turn us away once we're on his doorstep" she said matter-of-factly.

"But we don't even know where he lives!" Nick protested.

Molly's face fell.
"Alright, that's true" she accepted. "But Calshot isn't a big place. If a visitor came along asking after your Aunt Clutterbuck here in Burley, most people would probably know of her.

We'll just ask around. What do you think?"

Nick sighed but felt a little spark of excitement at the thought of a day trip and getting out of Burley for a change of scene.
"Okay" he relented. "Do you think they have any games arcades?" His eyes grew almost as wide as the grin on his face.
"I doubt it. We don't have time for games, anyway. We've got work to do"
"But how are we going to get there, given how notoriously bad the public transport is round here?"

"It's about a 2 hour cycle if we want to hire bikes…" Molly began, before seeing the disparaging look on Nick's face. "Oh I remember, you used to live five minutes away from the Tube station, and you don't do walking or cycling" she rolled her eyes. "Trains and buses are no good; there would be too many changes. If we're lucky there might be a coach trip coming up soon – lots of them go direct from here."

"But will your mum let you go?" Nick suddenly saw a flaw in the plan. "It's a long way for us to go alone"

"I suppose so" Molly said doubtfully. "I'll ask her, but I'm sure it will be fine. What about your aunt?"

Nick was fairly sure she wouldn't mind; besides, she was so absent-minded and engrossed with her cats that she probably wouldn't notice if he disappeared for the day anyway.

As it happened, the opportunity for a trip came far sooner than expected. When Molly asked her mum for permission to go, Lilianna had been reluctant at first.

"I don't know, Molly" she had said, drumming her long, purple fingernails on the kitchen counter. "It's a long day out for you two to be away by yourselves. What did you say you wanted to do there anyway?"

"Umm, see the coast and the…castle, and just have a look around. We've never been there before, have we mum?" Molly guiltily shifted from one foot to the other, but knew she couldn't reveal her intention to visit Lawrence.

"No we haven't, but isn't there anywhere closer you could go? What about Ringwood?"
"There's nothing to see in Ringwood, and we go there all the time" Molly complained.
"Nick, has your Aunt agreed to this?" Molly's mother asked. He shuffled awkwardly and replied in the affirmative; he wasn't really lying, he reassured himself, as he knew she would agree.

"Well, I suppose it should be alright" Mrs Morgan agreed grudgingly. "But hang on a moment – I think I remember a coach brochure coming through the letterbox the other day."
She began rifling through the drawers, turning up papers and notes of all kinds along with a bunch of basil, half a candle and a red ribbon.

“Ah, here we are!” she exclaimed, brandishing a battered booklet. “There’s a coach trip from Burley to Calshot, free for under 16’s. Well would you believe it, it’s tomorrow!”

“So can we go? Please?”

“Well…alright then. Seeing as you’ll be with a group it should be safe enough, as long as you promise not to stray too far away from the others and remember to get back to the coach in good time at the end of the day.”

Nick and Molly were triumphant. Maybe tomorrow would hold the answers to their questions about Rachel Morgan and the events of 1940.

1990
Molly

Hardly daring to believe our luck in securing mum's agreement and finding a method of transport to take us straight to Calshot, we waited at the coach stand the next day in high spirits. We had each been given a bit of money for lunch and ice cream, so all we had to do was find Lawrence. When the coach arrived, we boarded it with trepidation. Nick had brought his Walkman and tried to listen to Alice in Chains on the way but I knew he was too excited to concentrate on music.

He looked out of windows at the passing countryside like a dog sticking its head out of the car, and seemed genuinely happy for the first time since he arrived – who would have thought a Londoner like him would get so enthusiastic about a trip to Calshot? Well, one who has been stuck in a small village in the forest for weeks I suppose.

The other travellers were a mix of elderly people who were disembarking elsewhere on route, a couple of families, and a group of teenagers our age who jumped off at the Activities Centre at Calshot Spit. The journey took less than an hour but it felt like forever, and our hearts soared as we rounded a corner and were treated to our first glimpse of the glistening blue of Southampton Water which fed into the Solent.

Boats bobbed in the marina and Calshot Castle stood sentinel over the Spit. I tried to give Nick a potted local history lesson, explaining that the castle was built by Henry VIII and that later on in the 1800s it was used as a base of operations for catching smugglers, but he didn't seem interested. His eyes were glued to the water.

"Haven't you ever seen the coast before?" I asked sarcastically. I didn't really think that anyone could have reached the age of 15 without going to the seaside, but it turns out he had.
"I've lived in the city all my life, I've only ever seen the Thames" he explained.
I regretted my harsh words and felt sorry that he'd never had the pleasure of that timeless childhood memory of a day at the beach, squealing as the tide rushes in higher and higher towards your toes at each sweep, the smell of sun cream mingled with seaweed, that grainy bite into a limp cheese roll which has somehow, inexplicably, become full of sand.

"You're not really selling it to me" he grimaced when I described it. "I'm glad we're not here for a day at the beach and we're just looking at it from a distance!"

We alighted from the coach near the Spit and stood there feeling a bit lost. I'm not normally one to be discouraged but my heart sank a little as I realised the enormity of the situation – we had no idea where Lawrence lived and hardly any notion of where to begin.

It was like looking for a needle in a haystack, and I felt foolish for insisting on coming here. I took a few deep breaths like mum always does when she's meditating, and inhaled the fresh sea air, my cheeks warmed by the gentle morning sun. I heard the distinctive cry of seagulls and looked up to see them wheeling overhead. Absorbing the sights and sounds for a moment, I gradually felt my usual optimism returning. I glanced over as Nick give a disdainful sniff.

"What's that smell?" he wrinkled his nose.
"That's the seaweed I told you about. You'll get used to it."
"I don't think I want to" he muttered, but I could tell he was pleased to be there.
"So what's next?" he asked.
"I guess we just walk around and get our bearings"
"We need a bit more than bearings. We need to find a 62 year old man who doesn't want anything to do with us, and we don't even have a clue what he looks like"
"I'm sure something will turn up. Things usually do, if you just go with the flow and see what happens"
"Riiight. So in the absence of any kind of plan whatsoever, we'll just wander around and hope we bump into him".
"Something like that."

We agreed there was no point asking at the Activities Centre; it was highly unlikely that Lawrence was a regular visitor to the climbing wall.

My mood dropped again when Nick voiced his doubts as to whether we'd even find him at home here in Calshot anyway; after all, he may be at work during the day if he wasn't yet retired.

After wandering around for a while, we happened across a sign for the Sailing Club. It was only a small wooden clubhouse hut but we thought it was worth asking in there. If Lawrence had chosen to settle in Calshot so near to the coast, it was possible that he also liked sailing or that at the very least, he might have been a regular sight walking up and down the waterfront.
Our footsteps made the wooden jetty creak as we neared the hut. Smartly painted yachts were moored proudly next to jauntily bobbing dinghies. It appeared deserted except for one middle-aged man dressed in a white jumper, sharply pressed shorts and deck shoes, exiting the clubhouse holding a rope and an anchor.

I moistened my lips with my tongue and cleared my throat nervously.

"G-good morning" I croaked.

"Good morning" he nodded, his crisp accent straight out of public school. "What can I do for you?"

I was grateful when Nick surprised me by smoothly taking over.
"We're on a day trip and we're looking for an old family friend who lives here, a Mr Lawrence Longley. Do you know him?"

"Of course I know him!" the man smiled, and if he was surprised that the two scruffy teenagers before him were friends of Lawrence, he didn't show it. "You know he works here, of course?"

We tried to hide our shock at hitting the jackpot so quickly and simply nodded.

"Well, we all know each other here in the sailing community" the man continued, perching his sunglasses on his head. "Lawrence is the treasurer and secretary of the club but he has a day off today so you'll no doubt find him at home or trundling in his garden. His honeysuckle is doing wonderfully, you know. You have his address, naturally?"

I swallowed, feeling horribly guilty, but thought to myself that in a way, he *was* an old family friend so it wasn't really a lie, just a stretching of the truth. He and my gran had evidently been close during the war when they were both evacuees, after all, so I forged ahead.
"Yes we do, but we've never been here before so we're not familiar with the roads. Would you be able to point the way?"

Fortunately, he didn't seem at all suspicious and was happy to explain.
"Certainly, certainly. It's not far at all, just walk up there along the waterfront, turn left and then after about 500 yards you'll see a row of white cottages – his is the one with all the delightful rosebushes at the front, you can't miss it."

We thanked him profusely and began following his directions, a knot of worry tangling tighter in the pit of my stomach with every step.

When we spotted the cottage we both started to lose our nerve. We'd been worried about not finding Lawrence at all, but now it had transpired to be straightforward, and we were actually *there* outside his front door, our courage was failing us. We hadn't really discussed what we would say or even what we hoped to discover, we'd just blindly jumped on the coach and travelled here in the vague hope that he'd welcome two complete strangers into his home and tell us everything we wanted to know. I felt ridiculous.

Trying to summon up the bravery to lift our knuckles to knock, things were taken out of our hands by a tall, grey-haired man who yanked the front door open crossly, having spotted us from the window.
"Yes? What do you want?"

"Mr Longley?" I asked querulously.

"Yes?" he snapped. "Who the devil are you? Oh, I know" he realised, suddenly placing my voice, and his brows knitted even more tightly together.
"You're the one who telephoned yesterday. You've got a cheek turning up here! What the hell d'you want?"

Nearly in tears with humiliation and frustration, I did my best to appease him.

"I'm very sorry Mr Longley. I know we shouldn't have come here like this. I'm Molly and this is my friend Nick Rivers. Rachel Morgan was my gran like I told you yesterday, and I really want to learn about her life as a child during the war. She died when I was young and she never spoke much about her childhood. You wouldn't talk to me over the phone, so I didn't know what else to do".
I looked down sheepishly at my feet.

He grunted and I was certain he was about to slam the door on us when he stopped suddenly, seeing my face properly for the first time.
"Good lord, you do look like her" he murmured. I felt a bit uncomfortable as he studied me so closely. After a moment he exhaled heavily and his expression softened slightly, although he remained unsmiling.
"I'll give you ten minutes, and ten minutes only" he said reluctantly. "Come in if you must. Take your shoes off first, I've just had these carpets cleaned".

Hardly able to believe our luck, we stepped inside without a second thought. When we pondered over the day's events later we realised it could have been a dangerous move to enter a strange man's house when nobody knew where we were. But somehow we felt it would be alright.

This was Lawrence Longley, who in our minds was still the bookish twelve year old boy who became friends with my gran during the war. We had known of course that he would be in his sixties now, but it felt funny to think this was the same person whom we had so far only really pictured as a child. So much time had passed that I suddenly doubted if he even remembered much from 1940 at all. Or if he did, perhaps he would simply be unwilling to tell us.

He grudgingly invited us to perch on his stiff leather sofa which creaked and squeaked beneath us. He didn't offer drinks and stood facing us sternly with his arms crossed.

"What exactly is it you want to know?" he asked, seeming a little intimidating. It was clear he was still sprightly, with his ram-rod straight back and athletic build; he was obviously an active member of the sailing community and he wore a polo shirt with a blue jumper tied casually around his waist emblazoned with the club logo.

"We found my gran's diary" I reminded him. "But it ended very abruptly. We read about… the witchcraft ritual in the woods, and that a woman named Margery Blackthorn was found dead the next day. We read that you both met Gerald Gardner and he asked you to get involved with something for the war effort. But then the entries stopped. What happened?"

Lawrence's face contorted into an expression I couldn't read. His brow furrowed.
"I told you on the phone that there's no need to go digging up the past. Why would you believe what's written in the diary of a twelve year old? What does it matter to you?"
"Mr Longley, I miss my gran very much and my mum was never told much about her childhood either. When I found her diary I was so happy to learn more

about her, but it raised more questions than answers. If she did something that contributed to the war effort, I want to have it acknowledged rather than kept secret."

Lawrence paused and looked as if he was about to give an angry retort, but then his lip quivered and he blinked rapidly a few times.

"What, er… when did your grandmother die?" he asked quietly, and Nick and I both looked up at him in surprise at his changed tone.

"In 1984" I answered. "I was 8 and she was only 56. It was cancer."
I peered at him quizzically, unsure of whether to continue. He stayed silent but I felt he wanted me to tell him more.

"She was so lively with sparkling eyes" I remembered. "Very talkative and friendly. But when she got ill, she became quieter and withdrawn.
I noticed it even though I was young at the time. And she would never say much about her life, she'd just clam up. I never really wondered why, until now. Anyway, she did suffer from illnesses on and off even before the cancer came. I think mum once said that she'd become ill when she was a child and never fully recovered, that she always seemed prone to infections and diseases".

Lawrence seemed to be fighting some kind of internal battle, and suddenly slumped down into an armchair with the appearance of a much smaller, older man.

Nick and I stayed silent, my own mind wandering back to those dark days after my gran had died and the world turned grey, stripped of its vibrant colours, drained of all life. I remembered the tense silences, the sudden unfriendliness of the hushed house, the days I felt like I was screaming inside but couldn't say a word.

Worst of all, the times when I almost forgot and rushed into the sitting room desperate to tell her about something silly; a ladybird I'd seen in the garden, the arrival of Miss Clutterbuck's new cat next door – little titbits that most adults would have found boring, but which my gran devoured, always wanting to know each and every detail, no matter how inconsequential. But of course, she wasn't there. For a long time after she died, I would hover around the corner imagining that if I just peeked round the door really, really fast then I might catch a glimpse of her sitting in her favourite chair once again, as if a little bit of magic and wishing could make her return.

"I'm sorry" Lawrence finally mumbled, visibly trying to gather himself. "It brings it all back, you see. I'm becoming quite a grumpy old thing, these days" a watery smile flickered on his lips. "I suppose you deserve to know the full story about what happened that year. I always missed her terribly you know, once the war was over."
"Did you both stay on at Mrs Fernley's until then?" I asked.
"Yes we did, for another five long years. In the absence of other family and friends, we grew up like brother and sister. But as with many siblings, the

disagreements and bickering escalated as we became teenagers. She became more and more carried away with witchcraft despite the danger and what had happened to her. I wanted nothing more to do with it and told her so. Eventually we grew apart and once we started forging our own paths as young adults in the post-war years, we just lost contact. But I always wondered. Thought about what she was doing, whether she was alright. Until you phoned yesterday, I had managed not to think of her for a long time, having mentally put the past to bed, so to speak. But now, seeing you sitting there and looking so very much like her…and you coming all the way out here uninvited to speak to me, well, it's just the sort of thing she would have done."

He trailed off and I felt sorry for him as he looked so vulnerable at that moment. I summoned up the courage to ask him a question.
"Mr Longley, you said that Rachel continued with witchcraft despite the danger and 'what happened'. What *did* exactly happen?"

He put a hand to his brow and sighed as though speaking had become a strenuous effort for him.

"Well, I suppose you'd better stay for a while longer and I'll tell you all about it".

Chapter 13

1940

The pure, white orb of a full moon hung in the sky; a glistening jewel illuminating the forest with an unearthly glow. Lawrence, Rachel and Mrs Fernley trudged through the foliage with fear in their hearts, praying that this time the ritual would be successful and they would all make it out alive. Rachel had recovered but was still a little weakened after the previous night's ordeal. It was unclear what exactly had happened and how it had affected her, and they could only hope that she wouldn't suffer any further symptoms after absorbing Thomas Wetherby's burst of negative energy.

Before they left the cottage, Mrs Fernley had entered Thomas's old study and stood gazing around for some minutes. On a whim, she picked up a small glass globe which appeared to be tinted with prismatic colours when you tilted it in the light. It was just an old knickknack that he had kept on his desk, but without really knowing why, she decided to tuck it into her skirt pocket for luck. She remembered one of the strange things he had said to her soon after they were married, which had always made her shiver.
"If I were to die" he had said earnestly, his dark eyes boring into hers, "will you promise to keep my things as they are? Don't throw any of them anyway, will you? Keep them safe."

She had brushed it off, admonishing him for being so silly and wondering why he would bring up something so morbid. But when he *had* died just a few years later, she had heard those words in her head replayed over and over, and she knew she would never move anything from his study. She never understood why, and over the years she had simply accepted that the room would never be used, and that was just the way it was. That was why she hadn't wanted to take Rachel on as her unexpected second evacuee; she had felt it was a violation of Thomas's memory for someone else to stay in there. But she needn't have worried as both Rachel and Lawrence had turned out to be good for her; despite her sharpness and lack of interest in children, she had found herself surprisingly pleased to have them around.

As she prepared for the night ahead, she pushed her maudlin thoughts away and brushed her fingers against the glass globe in her pocket for reassurance – she supposed it didn't really matter anymore about religiously keeping everything the way it had always been. She might even die tonight herself.

When they finally arrived in the clearing, the grim faces of the other participants reminded each of them yet again of the risk they were taking. Some of the enthusiasm of the previous night had dissipated, replaced with an edgy, grim determination. This time, everyone knew it was quite literally a case of 'do or die'.

Forming the circle as before and pacing round and round to the rhythmic hums and chants, Rachel and Lawrence felt the now familiar thrumming, pulsing energy racing through them. Mrs Fernley's face was full of concentration, and her body jolted as she sensed the power coursing through her. She threw herself into it with abandon, no longer able to yield to any scepticism, understanding that her complete belief and participation might be their only defence against the evil spirit that was once her husband. Unwilling to accept it, but unable to ignore the evidence before her, she cried out as she saw a dark presence rising in the centre of the circle. Her terror-filled eyes darted left to right and she realised that the others were writhing in pain and seemed to be engaged in some sort of mental struggle, just as they described last night, but none of them were aware of the figure growing before their eyes. A black, swirling mist was spiralling urgently, silent and menacing. Amongst the mist, she caught a glimpse of a man's face. A face she recognised. Closing her eyes and praying that she was mistaken, she nearly screamed as something clutched her shoulder and she felt her eyelids being forced to open against her will.

"Wilhelmina" a silky voice drifted into her ear and she jumped, still clinging desperately to the hands of the people on each side of her in the circle.

Thomas Wetherby stood before her, his face pale and flickering in its lack of solidity, his body shrouded in black.He seemed to be floating above the ground. In the back of her mind, Mrs Fernley was relieved that he had appeared as they had hoped, and had even

recognised her despite their initial doubts.
But the hardest part was yet to come, and her heart ached at seeing him once more after so many years.

"Why are you doing this?" she struggled to force the words out, still held in his grip although nothing physical appeared to be touching her.

"Doing what, Wilhelmina?" he hissed. "Giving back to the country the pain they gave to me? I lost my father to the war. So many others have been lost to war. War, war!" his voice rose and Mrs Fernley shrank back.

"I refused to fight" he continued. "And I was killed for it. Murdered! Because they were so happy to march towards death in the name of patriotism, and wanted everyone else to do the same. Why should they win now?"

"I understand" Mrs Fernley gave a choked whisper. "I do. But you must see, Thomas, if you stop the Cone of Power, it will lead to even more death and destruction. If we can prevent Germany's invasion of England, the war may be over more quickly, and fewer people will be lost."

Thomas spat, derision twisting his features and rendering them barely identifiable.
"There will be plenty of German loss of life though, won't there? Are they worth any less? War has ruined so much and always will. The British government must be taught a lesson they won't forget, for all the men who were killed in the Great War, and for those

like me who were ostracised for refusing to take part in their pathetic battle games."

Mrs Fernley forced herself to tear her eyes away from his face and was horrified to see that the others in the circle were still fighting the unseen force. She felt the hand of her neighbour twitch in pain and knew they couldn't hold out for much longer.

"What are you doing to them?" she summoned the energy to shout, her voice weak.

Thomas threw back his head as if in merriment. "Lord, what fools these mortals be!" he gave a deep, eerie, laugh that made her chest constrict. Her heart felt so cold, so tight. Her knees quivered.

In that moment, she knew that as Gerald had warned her, he wasn't really Thomas at all; there was barely a shred of him left. Suddenly his laugh ceased and his dark eyes roved around the circle and he sniffed, sensing something.

"What do you have in your pocket?" he barked. Mrs Fernley was taken aback for a moment before she remembered the small glass globe.

"It's just a silly little glass thing from your desk" she panted. "Listen to me, you *must* stop what you're doing, or you will kill everyone here in this circle! How can you claim to be against war when you so frivolously discard these lives?"

She gasped as she felt movement in her pocket and the glass globe began to float towards Thomas who still hovered ominously in the centre of the circle.

“I told you….not….to take *anything,* ANYTHING from my study!” he roared. At that moment, Gerald Gardner, still clutching the hands of his neighbours to retain the protective circle, opened his eyes and a sudden bolt of energy spun towards the globe, an aura of blue light all around him.

“We must smash it!” he cried out. “Wilhelmina, it must be destroyed! That globe is where he’s keeping his spirit. It’s dark magic - he must have cast a spell before he died, allowing him to return and cause havoc. If we destroy it, we defeat him!”

Thomas emitted a low, guttural shout and flung out his own bolt of energy. The globe hung in mid-air, caught between the powers of the two men.

“That’s why you didn’t want me to move anything from your study!” Mrs Fernley exclaimed, knowing she must keep talking. “You knew I despised your love of witchcraft, and that was even before I discovered you were dabbling in *dark* magic!
You suspected that if you told me what you had done, I would have destroyed the globe and that would have been the end of you and your evil spirit. You used such an everyday object that nobody would know”

Thomas glanced back at his wife, still concentrating on supporting the globe with his power.

“Shut up!” he roared, the dark mists swirling about him in turmoil as he fought to retain control.

Gerald grunted with the exertion of preventing Thomas getting his hands on that small glass object upon which so much hung in the balance.

Mrs Fernley wrestled with her conscience for a moment before realising she had to do something to distract Thomas so that Gerald could destroy the globe. Keeping secrets didn’t matter anymore. If she didn’t do something, they could all die.
“You may not care if we lose the war!” she cried out. “You mightn’t even mind killing most of us here in this circle, including me. But do you realise that your own… granddaughter is here?”

Thomas’s bolt of energy fizzled out as his head snapped up in surprise. That split second was all it took for Gerald to take advantage of the lapse in concentration. Gerald’s bolt of light hit the globe with force, smashing it into a thousand pieces.

Thomas screamed. A haunting, heart-stopping scream which made them all desperate to clap their hands to their ears, but they knew they had to keep the circle whole.

They could only look on in amazement, relieved that their pain and the invisible stifling grip had been eased, watching as the evil presence spun round and round and round, the dark mists eating up more and more of the figure at each turn until there was hardly a shred left.

As the entity finally disintegrated before their eyes, they caught one last glimpse of the face of Thomas Wetherby. His eyes darted towards each of them in panic, frenziedly seeking the truth of Wilhelmina's words. A granddaughter. His eyes lit on Rachel. He smiled, showing a fragment of the man he had once been so long ago, and then he disappeared. A faint yellow wisp of something like smoke flew up and around the circle, and Rachel, in complete bafflement, felt sure she could hear a word being whispered over and over again. "Granddaughter. Granddaughter. Granddaughter", becoming quieter and quieter each time until the wisp of smoke and the susurrating murmur melted completely away.

Mrs Fernley slumped in exhaustion, blinded by tears. Rachel and Lawrence were breathless, conflicting thoughts racing through their minds, elated that Thomas Wetherby was gone but with so many questions still to ask. The faces of the others were pale and careworn, and nobody spoke. The silence reigned for only a moment before Gerald took control once again.
"We must continue" he said simply.

They all understood that for now, the questions would wait. They were free to finish what they had started and they must continue to propel the Cone of Power towards Germany. Summoning every last shed of energy, digging deep into their hearts and souls to somehow find the power they needed, they all projected their thoughts as hard as they could. Imagined the horror and disappointment the Germans would face if they tried to cross the Channel.

Pictured the fury of Hitler as he learned of the failure. Visualised the bereft families of soldiers attempting the suicidal mission. They projected the images with all the strength they could muster, feeling their combined power growing in intensity. Lawrence was struggling to breathe, wondering when it would all be over, wondering when they would know if it had worked. Suddenly, there was a change in the atmosphere, and they each felt a shift as though something had clicked into place. Rachel gasped as images popped into her head like a film reel, just like last time but stronger, more colourful, more powerful. British and, somehow - *American* soldiers dancing in the street with civilians, the sound of laughter, the flapping of bunting in the breeze. An overwhelming sense of joy and peace.

And then it was over. An unspoken understanding fell upon the members of the circle. It had worked.

Chapter 14

1990

"So that's what happened" Lawrence finally finished, sinking back into his chair as though totally spent. Nick shifted in his seat and blinked, almost surprised to be back in Lawrence's living room in Calshot, as the story had felt so real it was as though they had been transported back in time. Molly's heart pounded from the exhilaration she had experienced as Lawrence had explained how it felt to be part of the circle.

"So… it worked." Nick whispered, awestruck.

"It did" Lawrence nodded. "Some would say it can't be proven. After all, it did take another five long, terrible years for the war to be over. But Germany never did invade England, did they? We couldn't have stopped the war completely or end it before it had run its course. Some things can't be changed, you know, no matter how hard you try. But we certainly made a difference."

He shook his head.
"Anyway, I'm sorry I wasn't willing to talk about it sooner. We grew up knowing how important it was to keep quiet, just like everyone did during the war – a lot of people who worked on top secret projects never told their families even decades after it was all over. And talking about it brings back painful memories. Still, I don't suppose it matters now."

“There’s one thing I don’t understand” Molly wrinkled her nose. “What did Mrs Fernley mean when she said that their granddaughter was part of the circle?”

Lawrence gave a small smile and leaned forward again in his chair, steepling his hands under his chin. “I don’t know if it’s my place to tell you” he began. “But I don’t see how it can be avoided now. It must be time for you to know. As Mrs Fernley explained to Rachel afterwards, she and Thomas Wetherby had a child, although sadly he died before he knew anything about it. When her child, a girl, was born, she had her adopted by a couple who lived in Portsmouth. She really felt that her child’s life would be better there, unknown and with a fresh start. You see, by that time, she had learned of Thomas’s leaning towards the darker side of magic, and although she didn’t know to what extent he was wrapped up in it, she knew something had been going terribly wrong with him. She was worried that a child of his would grow up to be the same. She didn’t know how she would tell her daughter about him and realised it would be hard to bring her up alone in a place where Thomas had been known and had met his untimely end. So for all those reasons, she did what she thought was best.”

“But… couldn’t she have moved away somewhere with her daughter? Started a new life somewhere else?” Molly asked, struggling to make the connections in her head.

Lawrence shrugged. “Who can tell?” he answered. “She felt terribly guilty about it but believed that she had made the right decision. Anyway, her daughter went on to have a child of her own – Rachel. Your grandmother. Fate works in mysterious ways, and it seems somehow fitting that Rachel ended up being evacuated to Burley quite by mistake and staying with *her* grandmother, Wilhelmina Fernley!”

Molly opened her eyes wide.
“So Mrs Fernley’s daughter is actually my great-gran, and Mrs Fernley herself is my great-great-gran!”

“That explains why Rachel stayed in the house after the war and how it’s still in your family today.” Nick pointed out.
Lawrence nodded. “Sadly, Rachel’s parents were killed a short time after the Cone of Power took place, when their street was bombed. It was devastating, but Mrs Fernley was grateful for an opportunity to finally put things right, and although she had never been reunited with her daughter, she could look after her granddaughter and give her the best life possible. She left the house to her when she died. She had become so fond of me as well that I firmly believe she would have asked me to stay with her too if I hadn’t been lucky enough to have a home and family to go back to after the war.”

“When did Mrs Fernley realise that one of her evacuees was actually her own granddaughter?” Nick asked.

“We questioned her about that afterwards” Lawrence replied. “She explained it was the time she asked us about our families over the dinner table. When Rachel said that her mother had been adopted, the pieces all suddenly fit. She must have subconsciously begun to suspect it already at that point – I think she saw a resemblance to Thomas Wetherby. Rachel had obviously inherited his dark hair and some of his facial features, rather than Mrs Fernley’s. It was a huge shock, I can tell you”.

All three of them were quiet for a few moments, lost in their own memories and reflections.

“It feels like everything has finally come right at the end” Molly mused. “It’s strange. It’s like a twist of fate that I live in Burley. If just one tiny bit of the past had been different, I might be somewhere else right now and have never known about any of this. But it makes me shudder a bit to think I’m also related to Thomas Wetherby.”

Nick pushed his hair out of his eyes thoughtfully. “But your ancestors don’t define you. Anyway, it sounds like maybe he saw the error of his ways at the very end, when Mrs Fernley made him see he was about to hurt his own granddaughter.”

“Tragically, it seems he already had” Lawrence said. “You know, I believe the reason Rachel was ill so frequently during her life and died of cancer, god rest her soul, was that burst of dark energy that flowed through her the first time we took part in the circle.

She *seemed* to go back to normal but it must have left a lasting impact; she was lucky not to have been killed outright like poor old Margery Blackthorn."

"It's an amazing family history" Nick said. "I'm glad I came here after all and heard about all this. Not that I've got anything to do with it really, just that I expect it was some relative on my mum's side as a Clutterbuck who was involved with witchcraft in the area, and maybe took part in the ritual too".

Lawrence chewed his lip and hesitated before speaking.
"I wonder if there's more to it than that".
"What do you mean?"
"What did you say your surname was, Nick?"
"Rivers. Why?"

Lawrence let out a long breath and paused before speaking.
"This might be a strange question" he began.
"But…during your time in Burley, have you ever seen a ghost or…experienced anything odd?"

Nick and Molly looked at each other.
"How did you know that?" he replied, astonished.
"There was one time when all the lights went off in Molly's attic. It sounds a bit silly now. But the most unnerving thing was the photo Molly took – when it was developed, we saw a man who looked like he'd stepped out of the 17th century. When we looked at it again later, he had disappeared".

Lawrence shivered.

"Funnily enough, Rachel and I saw him too. There were a couple of odd happenings while we were staying with Mrs Fernley; feeling someone brush past, you know the sort of thing. Something that really terrified us was when Rachel was larking around outside in a thunderstorm. She said she felt a hand push her out of the way moments before a bolt of lightning hit the ground where she had been standing. One particular evening, believe it or not, a ghost actually appeared in Mrs Fernley's parlour right in front of us - Molly, I expect you know the story of Jeremiah the smuggler?"

Molly nodded. "Of course. I was telling Nick about that the other day. We did think it could be his ghost who appeared in our photo".

"I have a feeling it might have been" Lawrence agreed. "After things had died down after the summer of 1940, I did some research and learnt a little more about the legend and I uncovered some further details about Jeremiah, who was most certainly a real person. Now this might be just a coincidence and I suppose it can't prove anything but… it's rather strange. Do you want to know what Jeremiah's last name was?"

Nick and Molly nodded, curious as to where this was going. Lawrence leant forward, eyes wide and whispered,
"It was Rivers".

1990
Molly

When Lawrence explained that the infamous local ghost Jeremiah had been a Rivers, Nick and I were baffled for a moment and not sure what to think. We knew that having the same surname is no guarantee of being related, but the coincidences were really starting to add up. It felt right somehow to believe that Nick was the descendant of Jeremiah the smuggler; after all, it was as if a twist of fate had led both of us to Burley as a culmination of chance events when otherwise things might have turned out very differently.

"I hate to interrupt the family reunion with bad news" I spoke reluctantly. "But we all know how the legend goes. Jeremiah is said to appear only to those who are in danger."

"Yes, exactly" Lawrence replied gravely. "With the dangerous events that followed, it's easy enough to work out why he appeared to us. Jeremiah's appearance certainly bore a warning message for Rachel. In fact, I wonder if he was there with us that night somehow. Perhaps if it weren't for his protection, it really would have been worse. But I wonder why he's showed himself to you?"

Nick sighed. "What are we in for next? My parents said we were coming here for a quieter pace of life! It's been nothing but trouble ever since I arrived"

I shuddered, fingers of ice clutching my heart. I didn't want to admit how unnerved I was, but I could see Nick was also troubled.

"Well, fate seems to have brought us both to Burley" I said with forced cheeriness. "We must be meant to be here. What could possibly happen?"

I regretted those words later.

We glanced at the clock and realised we'd taken up enough of Lawrence's morning, so we thanked him profusely for telling us the story and in contrast to his grouchy demeanour when he first greeted us, I'd like to think he seemed a little disappointed that it was time for us to go. It was a while before we had to catch the coach home, and Lawrence suggested that we visit Luttrell Tower.
"It's a fascinating place" he explained. "We've got our own smuggling stories here too, you know. It was built in 1780 for Temple Luttrell, who was a member of parliament and reportedly a gentleman smuggler. There's a genuine smugglers' tunnel running from the cellar to an exit just above the beach and it would have been used for safely transferring contraband to and from Isle of Wight ships".

As we put our shoes back on and got ready to leave, I saw that the walls were adorned with framed artwork which I must have been too nervous to spot on the way in. I admired a dramatic seascape with a lighthouse moodily standing guard in the background over a roiling, stormy sea.

“This is brilliant” I said. “Did you paint all of these?” “As a matter of fact, I did” replied Lawrence, pleased that I’d noticed them. “I’ve been drawing and painting for as long as I can remember. It really kept me going during those first months in Burley. Your gran gave me a sketchbook you know. I’d left mine at home and she spent her whole five shilling postal order from her parents on it.” He smiled, lost in the memory.

Something suddenly made sense. “We found a picture in the attic” I told him. “It was a tiger. *You* must have drawn that. Right?”

“Yes, I did.” He looked into the distance wistfully. “I remember that one well. I drew it for Rachel as a way of thanking her for the sketchbook. I thought it would remind her of her uncle who fought in India. So she kept it all those years!”

“Of course she did” I said. “I know she would never have forgotten you”.

Bidding a regretful farewell to Lawrence who somewhat shyly muttered that he “wouldn’t mind too much” if we wanted to visit again, we decided to quickly grab a sandwich from the local shop and then wander over to the tower which was less than half an hour away on foot.

It wasn’t hard to spot; a tall, yellow-brick, stuccoed folly rising up to the clouds, a smaller separate turret reaching up even further into the clouds.

I squeezed my eyes shut and imagined myself there in the 1700s on a dark, rainy evening, feeling the spray from the Solent hitting my face and the chill of the coastal wind whipping my hair. Hearing the calls of smugglers as they heaved casks along through the dark, dank tunnel. Feeling the unease they must have experienced each time they risked their lives, wondering whether the next thing they would hear would be the shot of a government man's musket, the acrid scent of gunpowder in their nostrils.

Opening my eyes and shaking myself back to reality, I looked up at the imposing edifice. Nick didn't understand my fascination, but I've always loved old buildings. After all, they might just look like bricks and mortar now but once upon a time, they were home to people and their stories, their joy and their grief, their excitement and their apprehension woven into the essence of the stones. Every place has its tales, and it was easy to envision the smugglers using the tall turret as a perfect vantage point for spotting their ships coming in.

It didn't take long to identify the entrance to the tunnel; perhaps all those hundreds of years ago it had been better hidden, but now it was simply of interest to tourists. A huge grey archway framed a smaller dark entry gate which would run from the beach into the tower.
"Can we go in this way?" asked Nick uncertainly.
"I don't know, but there's no sign saying we shouldn't."
Always eager to explore, I stepped into the tunnel without a backward glance.

It was chilly in there away from the sun and it smelt dank and musty. Moss lined the walls and the tunnel twisted and turned ahead into the darkness. There was only room to edge along single file and I thought how claustrophobic it must have been for smugglers hurrying through with their barrels, wondering if they would somehow be caught at the other end, emerging from the darkness straight into the gunpoint of an excise man.

After a few moments, I froze and Nick bumped into me, nearly sending us both tumbling over.
"Sorry" I hissed. "I thought I heard something. Listen!"

We pricked up our ears and sure enough, we could hear the gentle background whooshing of the waves.

"Where's that coming from?" Nick asked, worried. "We're going away from the beach surely, not towards it."

We waited a moment, realising that the sound was getting louder all the time. A thought struck me and my blood ran cold.

"It sounds like the tide is coming in" I whispered. "How could it have risen so quickly? It wouldn't have come all the way up the beach already, would it?"

"We'd better go back" said Nick. "Come on, let's turn around and get out of here."

We carefully rotated and were about to start walking back down the tunnel when we saw a rivulet of water lapping at Nick's trainers.
"What's happening?" he whimpered.

"Don't panic" I reassured him. "The tide can't have risen that much yet, and in the worst case we'll just end up wading through a couple of feet of water. No problem."

Nick looked unconvinced. "I hope you're sure about this" he said, and he must have been genuinely scared because in the last few minutes he hadn't once flicked his hair out of his eyes in his habitual way.
"I hate water and I can't swim" he admitted. "It's alright to look at from a distance, but I don't want to get close".

"Trust me" I said, grabbing his hand. "I've been to the beach enough times to know that the tide doesn't come in so quickly that we'd be cut off – we're not that far down the tunnel from where we came in. Let's get a move on."

We made our way back towards the beach, walking as quickly as the narrow walls and lack of light would allow. The sound of the waves lapping around our trainers made our hearts beat faster. Despite my reassuring words, they seemed to be getting increasingly persistent and reaching a little further up our feet with each sweep. We emerged from the tunnel with a sigh of relief; as I'd suspected, although the tide had come in unexpectedly swiftly, there was no need for us to swim our way back to dry land.

The sun had disappeared and fat drops of rain began to plink down around us from a grey sky bulging with clouds. You know, the British are often accused of talking too much about the weather, but that's because it's so darned *changeable*. Just minutes before it had been a warm, bright day and the contrast was unnerving.

But still, we were safely out of the tunnel.
"See?" I said with a smile. Nick grinned back with undisguised relief and we were just about to head back to the main road when a cry made our blood run cold.

"Help!"

We looked at each other.

"Where did that come from?" I said, my voice quavering.
"Sssh. Listen" Nick replied.

I was hoping and praying that we'd been mistaken, but within a moment or two another plaintive cry rang out.

"Help!"

"My god" Nick said, turning to me in horror. "It's coming from the tunnel! There must be someone else in there, trapped further inside!"

My stomach flipped. You know how in books people say that they 'felt their blood ran cold'?

I always thought that was a pretty silly phrase, but now I realised it's actually a pretty accurate description of what happens when genuine horror strikes you.

Our eyes searched the beach in panic, hoping to spot someone who might be able to help, but we knew it was fruitless – Calshot wasn't really a place people went to swim so there wouldn't have been a lifeguard. The area seemed deserted, as everyone must have retreated back indoors when the rain started. It was falling faster now, and the incoming tide was insistent and ferocious, the sea bubbling and stormy. The wind lashed us with biting ferocity and all traces of the once summery day had fled.

"Should we run to the sailing club and see if that man from earlier is still there, the one who told us where Lawrence lives?" Nick was forced to raise his voice over the now roaring wind and waves. "He might be able to help!"

I shook my head firmly.
"There isn't time" I decided. "We'll have to go back in there ourselves."

I started running back towards the tunnel before my nerves could make me change my mind. My instincts took over, salty spray flicking up into my face as I splashed through the encroaching water.

I didn't expect Nick to follow me; after all, he couldn't swim and I thought he might decide to go and get help while I went inside, but I heard his frantic footsteps behind me within seconds and felt his hand on my arm.

"Wait" he panted. "I'm coming with you". For once, there was no humour in his voice and I almost wished he would come out with one of his wisecracks. When Nick is this serious, it means things really must be bad.

With no time to show my gratitude, we hurried back into the tunnel which was rapidly filling with water. The walls deadened the sound of the crashing waves in the distance, but the water persistently lapped further and further up to our ankles, then to our shins, then ever higher until it was nearly at our knees.

The calls were still coming from inside.
"Help! Help!"

The sound spurred us on. As we rounded a slight bend in the tunnel, I caught my shoe on a protruding stone and tripped. I reached out to break my fall, fingers brushing against slime and moss. Nick's steadying hand was there to help me stand up straight again, and we continued our frenzied descent ever further into the tunnel.
"Hello?" I shouted. "Where are you? We're coming!"

"We're here! Help!" the whimper sounded closer now, and we made out two small shapes in the darkness.
Breathing hard, we reached the very end of the tunnel, marked by a huge oak door which presumably led into the Luttrell house.

Crouched in front of it were two young children who couldn't have been much older than six.

"Are you alright? What are your names?" I knelt down to their level, hearing my piston-pumping heart in my ears. I saw that they were identical twin boys, both with grubby tear-stained cheeks and looks of terror, evident even in the tunnel's gloom.

"I'm Ted, and my brother's Trevor" one said tremulously. "We were in the house with mum and dad. The door was open so we went in when they weren't looking and saw this tunnel. Then the door closed behind us and we can't get back in".

I realised that they had probably been holidaying at the Luttrell house with their parents, as I'd heard it was now available to let; families could pay to stay in the tower while they visited the area. I now heard a muffled banging from the other side of the door – it was too thick for the sound to travel through properly, but I imagined it must have been their parents struggling to get it open from the other side, having realised their sons were trapped.

"The water's rising" Nick whispered to me, not wanting to startle the children any more than they already were. With panic, I saw that the level had climbed almost up to their chests.

"Quick, let's try and get the door open from this side".

We both heaved and pulled, but it was wedged firmly shut. It was obviously designed to be heavy duty enough to keep the water out of the house in case the tunnel ever flooded like this.

“What are we going to do?” I panted. “It’s too late to turn back and take them all the way through the tunnel to the beach – the water will have risen too high and we’ll be trapped. They won’t be able to swim, and you can’t either – especially not while carrying the boys.”

I touched my ruby Leo amulet which I had taken to wearing on a string around my neck. It gave me a glimmer of reassurance but whatever power it had, it certainly wasn’t going to be enough to save us. All we could do was pick up one child each to keep their heads above the water. The level was creeping ever higher and it was now up to our own waists. It felt cold and heavy around our legs and it chilled us to the bone. It was at that point that I genuinely thought we might not make it out of there alive. My head filled with thoughts, memories and dreams and my eyes roved desperately, looking for a solution to appear, or a way out we had somehow missed, even though I knew there wouldn’t be. Nick was clearly just as scared as I was, his face drawn and his hands shaking as he held Trevor. He kept coughing, which I guessed was due to his weak chest after the bronchitis he’d told me he had last year – the cold water must have been affecting him.

“You know” I had a sudden urge to confess, “The day you first arrived in Burley, I didn’t like you much. I

imagined you tripping and ending up face-first in Miss Clutterbuck's trifle".
I eyed him sheepishly and was gratified to hear him laugh, although it was followed by a fit of coughing.

"Thanks for that" he spluttered. "Anyway, I'd far rather be face down in a bowl of trifle than standing here about to drown at any moment. So what do you think of me now, then?"
"Oh, you're alright I suppose." I gave a weak smile which he returned. "Anyway, I'm sorry I thought that about you."

"Well, I wasn't too sure about you at first either" he admitted. "I assumed you would be boring and naïve after growing up here all your life, and your defensiveness about Burley was annoying. But" he went on, "I realised I was wrong almost straight away. Boring? Ha! Since I arrived, life has been anything BUT boring. It was your madcap idea to come here today, don't forget!"

We were both just teasing, feeling that it was the only thing we could do under the circumstances to distract ourselves from our imminent doom. The boys had become horribly silent, so far beyond fear that they were no longer even crying.
"Don't worry, Ted" I muttered as reassuringly as I could to the twin I held in my arms.

And it was then that something strange and miraculous happened. I blinked once, twice, to make sure I was really seeing what I thought I was seeing, and not a near-death hallucination. The air shifted

and flickered, and a man appeared in front of us.
He was insubstantial, glimmering a little.
He was dressed in the clothes of an old-fashioned smuggler, although we could only see his top half due to the now chest-high water, but the waves shifted around his middle as if he was causing an air disturbance.

We knew immediately that this was Jeremiah Rivers, the man from the photograph. The man who had sacrificed himself in the 1700s to allow his friends to escape. The man who was Nick's ancestor, and the man who had warned my gran and Lawrence of danger in 1940 and had maybe even protected them from worse harm during the ritual. My gaze was fixed on Jeremiah, but I knew without looking that Nick's mouth had fallen open like mine.

"It is exactly 50 years to the day since last I appeared" Jeremiah spoke, his clear and solid voice belying his ghostly appearance. "I was needed then, and so I am needed now" he continued.
His eyes met Nick's and I saw recognition there. He glanced at me too and nodded. "The wheel has come full circle: I am here. But I am no longer strong enough, and the next fight cannot be mine".

Then he turned to face the heavy oak door. His form appeared to fade in and out of focus, and then there was a click, and slowly, slowly, the door began to move.

Within seconds, the boys' parents on the other side had taken the opportunity to yank it open fully and water was gushing from the tunnel into the house and we were almost knocked over in the sudden flurry. As we handed the children over to their distraught parents who were crying with relief, I looked back. Jeremiah had disappeared.

Chapter 15

1990
Molly

After the door opened and the sea flooded through into the Luttrell house at the pace of white water rapids, nearly knocking us off our feet, we were relieved, sodden and exhausted. We were ushered inside and managed to pull the door closed to stop more water gushing in. The carpet in the corridor was ruined, but that was the least of anyone's worries.

We were safe, the boys were safe, and we were going to make sure that nobody made the same mistake again – the owner was horrified and assured us that signs would be mounted on the internal door to warn people of the danger, as well as on the outer beach entrance along with a daily timetable of the tides.

Neither Trevor nor Ted had seen Jeremiah, but then their eyes had been squeezed tightly shut at the time. Their parents had been frantically tugging at the door from the inside and when it had finally succumbed and clicked open, they assumed they had just finally managed to dislodge it. If we'd told them what really happened, I don't think they would have believed us. But Nick and I know it's true.

Once the furore had died down and the boys' parents thanked us profusely, we realised we had long since missed the coach, so we had to call mum on the phone in the lobby of the Luttrell house.

She was so relieved that we were safe when we explained what had happened that she wasn't at all annoyed about having to come and collect us. Nick's aunt came with her, and she had brought along two bowls of trifle to help us 'recover after the ordeal' as she put it, which was a nice thought but she'd forgotten the spoons. They had lined the back seats with old towels as we were still sopping wet – every time we lifted our legs they felt heavy and saturated, and when we took off our shoes and emptied them, it seemed like half an ocean's worth of water came pouring out. The smell of seaweed lingered for quite some time, reminding us of our escapade.

When we talked later about the startling events, we realised the truth of what we had mused over earlier at Lawrence's house – how strange it was that we had both ended up here through various twists of fate. We weren't sure why or whether a reason would become clear in the future, but it was an undeniable stroke of luck that we had taken a trip to Calshot that day and found ourselves in the tunnel just in time to save the boys. Although Jeremiah was our real saviour, it was clear that if we hadn't been there to hold them up above the water level, they would very likely have drowned.

But on the way home, a thought had stuck in my mind, about something Jeremiah had said before he disappeared.

"What do you think he meant?" I asked Nick, fiddling with my amulet in worry. "Did you hear him say that he's not strong enough, and that the next fight must be ours alone, or something like that?"

Nick nodded solemnly. "I was hoping I'd misheard" he grimaced. "Is it just me, or does that sound very, very ominous?
"Yep." I replied with a sinking heart. "And at this point, nothing would surprise me."

We still weren't entirely sure how to explain all the eerie occurrences of the last few weeks. Jeremiah's ghostly appearance in the photograph was clear, but we both had a funny feeling that there was something else going on. We hadn't forgotten the 'power cut' in the attic, the ominous feeling that went with it, and our shivers as the cassette tape juddered. It was a small enough incident in its own right, but in light of the events that followed and Jeremiah's new warning, we were pretty certain that it meant something.

"You mean like a malevolent ghost?" Nick looked disbelieving. "Jeremiah is a friendly ghost who protects us, so are you saying there's an evil one after us at the same time?"

I wasn't quite ready to voice my concerns, but I was convinced that the flooding in the tunnel was unnatural. I was absolutely sure that the tide couldn't possibly have risen so quickly, but nobody else at the scene had commented on it, probably wrapped up in the safety of the boys and overwhelmed with relief. I had a horrible feeling that something was trying to harm us - perhaps it had been trying its luck when it realised we were at the tunnel and the boys were trapped inside. But now that initial, simple attempt had failed, *it*, whatever *it* was, was going to try again sooner or later.

I shot him a look. "You can be sceptical if you want, but you can't deny everything that's happened up until now. It's a possibility, isn't it?"

He swallowed hard. "I know" he admitted. "I wish I *didn't* believe it, and a few weeks ago I would have said you were crazy. But you're right. So what do we do now?"
"I suppose all we can do is wait."

As it happened, we didn't have to wait too long. The rain continued that night, pelting and pounding on the roof like the cloven-hoof steps of a hundred demons, the gale rattling the window frames and howling like a banshee's warning. A storm so severe was unusual for this time of year, and I lay awake amid the alarming sounds, praying that there wouldn't be another power cut as I noticed my bedside lamp wavering. It was clear that despite my exhaustion, sleep wasn't going to come easily. I climbed out of bed and tiptoed gingerly over to the window to watch the thrashing trees lit by the dim glow of the streetlamp. I peered to the left towards next door and noticed the glow of a bedroom light – I suspected Nick was suffering from just as sleepless a night as I was. There was a blinding flash of lightning and instinctively I started counting. Most kids counted one-elephant, two-elephant but when I was little my mum taught me to say one-wicked-witch, two-wicked-witch, three-wicked-witch, four-wicked-witch, five-wicked- I stopped as the rumble of thunder reached my ears. Five seconds for the sound waves to travel - that meant the electrical storm was about a mile away. I hoped it wouldn't get any closer.

Shivering with cold, I turned to get back into bed. A sudden, insistent, thumping rumble directly overhead made me call out with shock – I hadn't even seen the lightning flash this time. How had it travelled so quickly? Trying to slow my rapid breathing, I told myself not to be silly.

I'd never liked thunder and lightning much, that grinding grumble as if someone were moving heavy furniture around in the sky. There was a flash of white light and my eyes jumped automatically back to the window. But it wasn't lightning. The glare remained, like a piercing white strobe etching a picture in the sky.
I blinked once, twice. It was so painfully bright I had to shield my eyes, but I couldn't help but recognise the image that had been created, burned like an afterglow into the sky. I'd seen it enough times in history lessons at school, in books and films. It was a Nazi death's head.

I was frozen to the spot, unable to move. I closed my eyes and counted, telling myself that if I just didn't look for five seconds, it would be gone. It was a bad dream, a hallucination induced by tiredness and the horrible events of the day down in the Luttrell tunnel. One wicked-witch, two wicked-witch, three wicked-witch, four-wicked-witch, five-

Another deafening thunder clash interrupted my frenzied counting, and I opened my eyes. The symbol was still there, but had now been joined by a red mist and a dark, black, swirling fog that formed as I watched into another symbol that had struck fear into the hearts of millions during the war. A swastika. The black fog was darker even than the night sky around it, with the red mist seething, draped around its edges like a bloodied robe. The rain and wind continued, but no amount of water could wash those pictures out of the sky, or out of my mind.

My eyes were drawn to a movement on the ground – a figure walking through next door's garden, stiff and uncertain, looking up at the sky. Nick!

I flung the window open and shouted as loudly as I could, as chill air and rain forced its way in, slapping at my cheeks.
"Nick! Nick! Where are you going? Get back inside!"

But the whooshing wind and the hammering rain drowned out my cries. I knew there was only one thing I could do. I had to go after him.

Grabbing my jacket and throwing it over my shoulders, I scrambled desperately for a pair of shoes. Finding them, I crammed my feet inside and pounded down the stairs to the front door. I wrestled to close it against the buffeting wind, and squinted in the dark through raindrop-beaded eyelashes.

"Nick!" I shouted, almost in tears of terror. I spotted him and ran as fast as I could to catch up, grabbing him by the shoulder.

He spun around, gasping in shock before realising it was me.
"What the hell are you doing?" I screamed. "Get back inside!"

He blinked and shook his head as if waking up from a trance, drenched hair plastered to his forehead.
"I don't know" he mumbled, confused. "I… felt like I had to get up and come outside. Almost as if…something was telling me to." He coughed, chest weakened again by the cold and damp seeping into his clothes.

He looked up, eyes widening as he noticed the evil symbols for the first time.
"What the -?"

"I don't know" I called, wincing as the bitter wind whipped at my ears and face, my saturated pyjamas chilling me to the bone. "But we need to get back inside. It's not safe out here!"

Suddenly, a bolt of lightning flung its way towards us, and before I could even think or make a conscious action, I whirled round automatically, holding up my hands in defence. I felt a jolt, a burst of scorching heat, and heard Nick shout. It took me a baffled moment to absorb what I was seeing. The lightning bolt had stopped in mid-air, apparently held off by a fizzing, green ball of energy coming from… coming from *my hands.*

"Get back" I whispered.

Nick, mouth open like a codfish, stepped behind me without a word, obviously thinking better of questioning anything at that moment. I felt tired and my arms were heavy, as if I was expending all my energy on holding off this shard from the sky. The swastika winked above us like a devil and I sensed that a further blast of energy would be coming.

"When I say 'now', drop to the floor and roll to the side" I hissed urgently.

I felt every fibre of my being cry out in exhaustion. Although I had absolutely no idea what I was doing or how I was doing it, I was sure I couldn't keep it up for long.
"Now!" I shouted.

Nick and I threw ourselves to the ground as I released the tension in my hands and the lightning bolt flashed where we'd just been standing and hit the bush behind us, catching it alight in a fearsome flare of flame.

"Get up!" I yelled, grabbing Nick's arm and dragging him to his feet. My thoughts were rapid and clear, some ancient, primal instinct taking over. I looked up at the sky. The Nazi death's head was directly above, a looming sentence of execution.

I sensed it before I saw it, another bolt flying down from the sky towards us. I threw up my hands and drew power from some unknown, hidden well within myself, summoning my green protective energy and stopping the bolt in its tracks. I kicked off my shoes, somehow knowing that if I grounded myself I would be able to draw more power from the sodden earth. Rain blurred my vision and the wind grew louder, deafening me to anything but the storm and the lightning as my hair whipped across my face. I wished I could reach up and touch my ruby Leo amulet which I'd forgotten to take off before bed, but even as the thought crossed my mind, I felt its glowing warmth against my chest and felt reassured that it was there, sensing that it was somehow giving me as much protection as it could, although I knew we'd need far more than it could offer.

"Give it up" came a sneering, laughing voice. You're not powerful enough. I'm not going to waste my time playing parlour games with children".

Trying not to break my concentration, I glanced around me but couldn't tell where the voice was coming from.

"There's no point looking for me" the deep, mocking voice came again. "You won't see me."

“What do you want?” I screamed.

An evil chuckle full of smugness and superiority reached my ears. “What do I want? I want to make you and your little friend disappear. You’ve been digging into affairs that are no concern of yours, and I don’t want you mincing around telling people about it. Your pathetic little idea that a group of witches could have helped to win the war, and thwart our invasion – you really believe it?”

My mind whirred as I struggled to keep my green energy alight. I didn’t know who this demonic being was, but I realised it must be the spirit of a long-dead Nazi.

“Yes, I do!” I screamed as loudly as I could. “And you know it’s true, or you wouldn’t care! You wouldn’t be trying to stop us! You *know* you were defeated, but you don’t want people to realise that YOU’RE the pathetic one. Who are you anyway? Some little-known war criminal who isn’t even named in the history books?”

I felt the lightning bolt pulse more forcefully against my defensive energy and knew I had angered the entity. Another bitter, booming laugh rang out and the ground vibrated beneath my feet.

“I could be Goebbels” he started singing in a mocking tone. “I could be Himmler. I could be Goering. I could be Hitler!”

"Who's the one playing children's parlour games now?" I replied as derisively as I could, determined to hide my fear.

"It doesn't matter who I am" he scoffed. "It doesn't matter if I admit it I suppose, as you won't live to tell the tale. Your kind defeated me in 1940. I was a witch working for the Fuhrer and it was my job to stop any attempts to enchant the High Command. I sensed Operation Cone of Power and tried to fight it. One of your own traitors even tried to do the job for me – Thomas Wetherby."

My look of surprise didn't go unnoticed as he continued, "Oh yes, I know all about him. Of course, he was too weak. I was in Berlin, detecting their attempts at the other end and staving them off. But the coven was somehow too strong for me. Me!" he spat.

"Those thought-waves were so effective that when I tried to warn our higher echelons that they had been tricked, they wouldn't believe me.
They thought their decision not to breach the Channel to invade England was theirs alone, based on logic and strategy. They didn't believe they had been influenced by a paltry pack of English witches. When I tried to persuade them for the good of the country, they thought *I* was the traitor against the Fatherland. I was executed".

He intoned these last words with undisguised venom. I wasn't surprised by the revelation that the Nazis had actually employed a witch to help them, thanks to what Nick had told me about Hitler and the occult the other day.

But as he had said, the only reason he was now admitting all this was because he intended to kill us. No-one would ever know; we were the only witnesses to his confession.
My muscles and mind were aching with the exertion of keeping the bolt away from us.

"We need to move again" I whispered to Nick, still standing silent behind me.
"Okay" he murmured back.

"Now!" I shouted, and once again we plunged to the side as I dropped my ball of energy and let the lightning bolt hit the ground harmlessly where we had been standing an instant before. The bush was still burning, the scorching, pungent scent filling my nostrils. It must have been an unnatural, magical fire, or the rain would surely have extinguished it by now.

"Why punish us?" I called up into the sky, regaining my feet and watching with apprehension as the death's head and swastika continued to glow ominously. "Your masters executed you. They were wrong. You were doing your best for your country and *they killed you.* Why take it out on us? We weren't even the ones to originally hold the ritual! We weren't even born then. We've done nothing to you".

Another bolt spun towards us in the blink of an eye, and I threw up my hands once more, panting with the exertion of holding it.

The owner of the disembodied voice was getting impatient.

"My countrymen did nothing wrong" it roared. "They were quite right to kill me if they believed me to be a traitor. I would have done the same thing. It was the fault of those old hags for bewitching them in the first place. My death was unimportant; what matters is they played a part in our downfall.
I haven't been strong enough to seek my revenge before now, but gradually my power has grown, reaching its zenith today on the fiftieth anniversary of that terrible day. As for you – I know you're the descendant of one of the witches involved. But I don't much care who you are - you've discovered what happened and I will never allow this shameful tale to be revealed and humiliate us. The world must never learn how we were defeated."

I was giving up hope of being able to hold the lightning bolt away from us for much longer. Dodging them only gave a temporary respite before the next one came shooting down from the sky. The evil entity had obviously tired of sending single bolts and now wanted to finish us off once and for all. I took a deep breath as I saw a flash and detected three bolts at once. I didn't know what to do. I closed my eyes and prepared myself for impact.

And then another miracle happened.

I didn't feel the burning, searing explosion of pain that I expected. I carefully opened one eye, and inhaled sharply as I saw the three lightning bolts suspended in the sky – one against my own glowing green hands, one being held off by my mum, and one being fought by Miss Clutterbuck. My heart leapt and sank at the same time; they were here to help, but that meant they were also both in danger.
Mum stood tall and powerful, her ethereal demeanour replaced with a determination that I could feel radiating from her from several feet away. Even wrapped in a dressing gown, she commanded respect. Thoughts flew threw my muddled brain – how did they know how to do this? Why hadn't they told me before? Why didn't *I* even know what I could do? I glanced gratefully at Nick's aunt, who also seemed to have grown from the small, eccentric character she normally presented. Her purple pyjamas and pink hair rollers, rather than looking ridiculous, seemed to add to her aura and personality. While mum loomed with an indescribable power and bearing, Miss Clutterbuck *glittered* with vitality.

The evil being was angry.

A massive thunderclap shook the ground and I wished I could squeeze my hands over my ears.

"What's this?" the booming voice jeered. "All friends together, are we? Well, friends who stand together *die* together too!"

"I don't think so" came a calm, steady voice. I nearly dropped my energy ball in shock as I turned to see a familiar figure walking towards us. It was Lawrence!

He must have taken the Nazi spirit by surprise too, as the three lightning bolts fizzled and fell uselessly to the floor. I took the chance to catch my breath, breathing rapidly with exhaustion.

"You!" it bellowed. "I know *you*" He laughed maniacally. "The time for revenge has indeed come."

Lawrence didn't flinch as bolts of power flew towards him. I heard a whooshing noise, and blinked as a protective blue bubble emanated from mum's fingers, forming a cocoon around him. The lightning bolts bounced off it and were sent firing back towards the swastika in the sky, rending it in two.

The spirit roared, although whether in pain or anger, I wasn't sure.

"What are you doing here?" Nick called out to Lawrence in the moment of silence that ensued.

"I sensed something this evening" Lawrence replied, standing straight and tall. "I couldn't shake off the feeling that something was wrong. I thought about what you said, about seeing Jeremiah, and I knew he must have been warning you of something terrible. I felt a force drawing me here, so I jumped in the car straight away. I knew exactly where to find you when I saw those evil signs in the sky."

“Can you and I help?” Nick asked him breathlessly. “You took part in the Cone of Power, even though you’d never done magic before. Can you show me what to do? Can we help them fight?”

“That’s exactly why I came” Lawrence nodded. “Quickly, we need to all join hands. Remember, as Ophelia said in Hamlet, we may know what we are, but not what we might be”.

Miss Clutterbuck and my mum hurried over, glancing at Lawrence in appreciation and agreement although they probably didn’t realise who he was.

There was no time for further introductions. The evil spirit had been gathering its power once more, and now let forth with a terrible inferno, billowing through the sky in our direction. I felt the unbearable heat, wincing as my eyebrows were singed and my lungs filled with smoke. The protective bubble was still holding but only just. Wordlessly, we somehow understood what we had to do. We began to hum and turn slowly in a circle, just like my gran and Lawrence had done in 1940 with the Burley witches.

The determination of Lawrence and Nick linked with the magic of my mum, Miss Clutterbuck and me, and I felt the power thrumming through me, electrifying and pure, so I could no longer feel the heat of the fire. I envisioned victory in my mind, summoning up images from the films I’d seen and the books I’d read, and even from Bedknobs and Broomsticks.

I imagined the Union Jack flapping triumphantly from a flagpole as the Nazi swastika fell torn and tattered into the sea. I imagined what the celebrations were like on VE day, the bunting hanging jauntily from buildings, the sweet taste of strawberries and cream, the laughter of soldiers who had returned, the jubilant but crackly voice on the radio announcing that the war was finally over. I felt it burning within me, bubbling up in success and triumph and pride. But I sensed it wasn't quite enough.
I knew that euphoria could only get us so far. I needed to feel *anger.*

Anger for the soldiers who had never returned, and for their families. Anger for the children whose young lives were torn apart by evacuation, or worse, by bombs. Anger for those empty desks in schoolrooms described by my gran in her diary. Anger for the pacifists who were met with injustice for standing up for their beliefs – even my misguided ancestor Thomas Wetherby. Anger for the downed Spitfires, the shrapnel wounds, the broken hearts and broken minds which would never again be quite whole. Anger not just for those in our country who suffered, but for everyone across the globe.
Anger for the communities destroyed by the Nazis, those sorrowful souls with hollow eyes and hollow bodies peering out from behind the bars of a labour camp with all hope gone. For the first time in my life, I let anger take over, boiling in my veins. I was angry on behalf of all who had been broken and lost in those terrible years, whose lives had been touched by war even in the smallest of ways.

I didn't think anything more miraculous could happen at that point. But as I felt the power flowing through me, through my hands to my friends and family in the circle, my eyes were drawn upwards and I felt an additional burst of energy.
I saw ghosts. Apparitions. Shadows of the dead – hundreds of the persecuted in their concentration-camp striped pyjamas, soldiers not just in British uniforms but German too. Men, women, children. I saw them flickering all around us in the sky.

My heart skipped a beat as I saw the man whom I somehow knew instantly to be Thomas Wetherby. And next to him – Gerald Gardner. Although I wouldn't have recognised them, I felt sure that Margery Blackthorn and Mrs Fernley, my great-great-gran, would be there too.

My heart warmed as I spotted Jeremiah amongst them– he had told us he wasn't strong enough for this fight, but he was still adding his ghostly power as best he could.
I wondered if the woman next to him with strikingly similar features could be his brave sister who had run through the night to warn him of the arrival of the excise men all those years ago in the 1700s.

The ghosts joined our humming and the sound rose to a fever pitch. The evil spirit's fire began to fade, and the being let out a roar of horror as the ghosts brushed their pale hands over the death's head and torn swastika in the sky, rubbing them out like a thousand erasers, wiping it from the heavens with their unity.

I gazed and gazed as the once haunted eyes of these sufferers began to glow with a spark of life even as their shapes remained transparent.

As the final strains of the evil voice ebbed away and the last tongues of fire spat their own elegies, and the burning bush fizzled out with no ceremony, I stared at the faces of those who had come to help us. They had come back for us, to help us drive the final nail into the coffin of the evils that had taken place decades ago.

As we remained clutching each other's hands in our circle, I sent them my thanks and gratitude with all my being. I looked up at them, and I knew they understood. I felt once again the raindrops on my face and began to notice my surroundings as we slowly returned to reality and the understanding that we were safe. The ghosts started to fade away; not sadly but with an air of contentment, as though they had completed the job they came to do.
And as I watched them swirling into the air, into the night sky which was now fresh and pure with no trace of the evil symbols, I saw gran amongst them. Rachel Morgan. I heard an intake of breath at my side and knew that my mother had seen her too. I looked to my right and saw Lawrence staring up at her with tears in his eyes. She smiled, warmth darting across her face for just one reassuring instant before she too faded away.

It was over.

Chapter 16

1990
Nick

Well, now I'm back to normal after lying in bed coughing for a week, Molly's letting me write a chapter from my perspective for a change, although it's the final one so naturally it's the hardest. She's already said it all, really, but she wasn't sure how to finish it off. Personally I think she was just worried what I might say about her if I had a few pages to myself, which is a bit of a cheek as she's written some unflattering things about me. Well, I might have mentioned the way she rarely shuts up and her infuriating habit of dragging us into trouble like the hare-brained trip to Calshot – but I'm glad it happened.

I haven't quite forgiven her for the trifle comment, but I must admit that anyone would be privileged to have her on their side, and she undeniably saved our lives by protecting us with her power. Anyway, she's given me strict instructions not to make any "wisecracks" in this chapter because it's meant to be a serious finale.

Although it's clichéd to round off with a nice, polished ending, that's really pretty much how it was. When we nearly drowned in the tunnel under Luttrell tower and Jeremiah, my however-many-times-great grandfather appeared, I could hardly believe my eyes.

I knew it was him straight away, and I felt sure I would have recognised him even if I hadn't seen the ghostly photo or discovered he was a Rivers – there was something uncannily familiar in his eyes and the set of his jaw.

Afterwards, I told Molly how admirable it was that she had raced into the tunnel like that, regardless of the danger. She gracefully replied that it was more admirable on my part, given that I couldn't even swim. I said no, I think it's called being stupid.

But my astonishment was greater still that night when we discovered why Jeremiah had appeared to warn us. As the bolts of lightning streaked towards us from the heart of the Nazi death's head, I thought it was the end. But Molly somehow drew power from within herself and from the earth, and her mum and my aunt did the same. I felt pretty useless until Lawrence made his timely appearance, and then I realised that despite our lack of witchcraft, we could help just by being there, by sharing our own human determination and strength – just like Lawrence and Rachel did during Operation Cone of Power. Turns out you don't have to be a witch to have powers after all.

I ran the whole gamut of emotions that night; fear, sadness, pity, strength, bravery, pride and happiness. Actually I'd say the 'fear' is more accurately described as sheer terror, but you know, I'm sure someone famous once said that you're not brave for doing something you're not scared of – real courage comes when you have to face up to something that petrifies you.

Once the evil Nazi spirit had been defeated, we all stood silently but joyously in the rain just relishing the feeling of being soaked to the skin, because at least getting wet meant we were alive. The rain had continued for a while but it was a natural, beautiful, refreshing rain, and the wind had died away completely. The only evidence that anything unusual had taken place there that night was the charred remains of Molly's mum's privet hedge. I had wondered whether anyone else had seen the symbols of evil in the sky, and how it would be explained. It turned out a few disgusted people did see it, and they blamed a far-right neo-Nazi group, assuming it was some sort of fireworks and trickery. That was perfect as far as we were concerned – they were questioned by the police and it even made it into the local newspaper, bringing the rest of the forest community together to denounce their despicable acts, and everything they represent. That particular group went quiet after that; they'd obviously received the message loud and clear that their prejudices were not welcome, so that was good news for everyone, as a by-the-way bonus.

A few days later, my parents phoned Aunt Clarissa to tell her that they had both received job offers in the area and the house purchase would be finalised within the next two weeks – a cottage just five minutes away from Molly and her mum.
My future in Burley secured, I started to settle in more and began to really think of it as 'home', even though I know I'll always miss the city. I rued the day I'd ever called Burley 'boring', I can tell you.

Now I can't imagine living anywhere else. We haven't witnessed any more ghostly experiences yet, and I hope we won't again, but it did turn out that the power cut in Molly's attic was simply due to some faulty wiring, so not everything can be attributed to the supernatural!

Lawrence returned home to Calshot with a renewed zest for life, and perhaps a little more respect for the path that Rachel Morgan chose – after all, although he had turned away from witchcraft he must still have kept an open mind and a little spark of something which allowed him to perceive that we were in danger that night, and to join hands with us in solidarity. We both see him as our honorary grandfather and we'll be visiting him regularly, but I don't think we'll be going back to Luttrell tower again in a hurry.

Sometime later, we managed to find Jeremiah's grave in the little village churchyard with Reverend Bumble's assistance. It was in the older section at the back, completely overgrown and almost reduced to rubble, but peacefully sheltered underneath a protective yew tree. We could just about make out the inscription:

Jeremiah Rivers
1746 – 1780
Beloved son, father, husband and brother
"A life of colour, zest and love,
Now at peace in heav'n above
We weep that He cut short your days
But know God works in mysterious ways"

As I tried to hide the tear that stubbornly escaped my eye despite my best efforts, and Molly valiantly pretended not to notice, I could have sworn I caught a waft of gunpowder and tobacco, but it drifted away as quickly as it had come.

We know that so many people played a vital part in winning the war; soldiers on land, air and sea, not forgetting those from other countries around the world who joined the fight, the Home Guard, the women's organisations, the people at home Digging for Victory, those who made important contributions in other ways like looking after evacuees and toiling away at the work that still had to be done in offices and factories up and down the country. Even those who fought on the other side should be honoured as while we may be divided by country, we are all the same in many ways, though we must never forget the atrocities committed against the many by the few. So although this story is about the specific contribution of the witches of Burley, and we truly believe there would have been a different ending without them, we are also grateful to every single person and animal who played their part, no matter how small – right down to the carrier pigeons who crossed the frontlines bearing crucial messages.

We wished we could tell people about our discovery of the difference the witches of Burley made to the outcome of World War II, especially as we didn't want to let the evil spirit's desires be granted and keep it from being revealed.

But despite our wish to let the truth out, we knew that society wouldn't yet be ready to understand or accept it, as even my own aunt had been reticent to tell us what she knew when we'd asked her about the events of 1940. So we decided that it should remain a secret for now, and Rachel Morgan's diary lies safe in Molly's attic where it was first discovered. Now you've read the story, we're trusting you to keep it secret too – you will, won't you? Maybe one day we'll know when it's the right time to uncover it again. We'll wait and see what lies ahead and which new stories will unfold in this wonderful green part of the world, rich with history and full of life, and what role we'll have in those stories in the future. After all, as Shakespeare wrote: "All the world's a stage, and all the men and women merely players. They have their exits and their entrances; and one man in his time plays many parts."

As for Jeremiah, Rachel Morgan and all the ghosts of war who stood with us, well - I have a feeling their work is done and we won't see them again. But it's okay. I know they're out there, watching over us.

The End

24615017R00145

Printed in Great Britain
by Amazon